OUTLAW GOLD

OUTLAW GOLD

Bradford Scott

CHIVERS
THORNDIKE

This Large Print book is published by BBC Audiobooks Ltd, Bath, England and by Thorndike Press®, Waterville, Maine, USA.

Published in 2006 in the U.K. by arrangement with Golden West Literary Agency.

Published in 2006 in the U.S. by arrangement with Golden West Literary Agency.

U.K. Hardcover ISBN 1–4056–3802–8 (Chivers Large Print)
ISBN 13: 978 1 405 63802 9
U.K. Softcover   ISBN 1–4056–3803–6 (Camden Large Print)
ISBN 13: 978 1 405 63803 6
U.S. Softcover   ISBN 0–7862–8726–8 (British Favorites)

The text of this Large Print edition is unabridged.
Other aspects of the book may vary from the original edition.

Set in 16 pt. New Times Roman.

Printed in Great Britain on acid-free paper.

British Library Cataloguing in Publication Data available

Library of Congress Cataloging-in-Publication Data

Scott, Bradford, 1893–1975.
    Outlaw gold / by Bradford Scott.
      p.   cm.
    ISBN 0–7862–8726–8 (pbk. : alk. paper)
    1. Texas Rangers—Fiction. 2. Corpus Christi (Tex.)—Fiction.
    3. Large type books. I. Title
    PS3537.C9265O94 2006
    813'.54—dc22
                                2006010235

ONE

The tall horse was black as the night itself, and that was Stygian, whatever the devil Stygian is. Anyhow, it was plenty black. Not a star in the sky. Not even the faint glimmer of a glowworm to relieve the gloom.

The horse didn't seem to mind it, for he ambled along sedately, the cheerful clump of his hoofs on the dusty trail blending with the moan and mutter of the water, also black, on his left.

Ranger Walt Slade, whom the Mexican *peones* of the Rio Grande river villages named *El Halcón*—The Hawk—leaned forward in his saddle and tried to peer ahead. But not even the eyes of El Halcón could pierce that ebon barrier which closed in on all sides, giving an effect of solidity.

'Shadow,' he said, 'darned if I don't believe you could cut it into chunks and build a wall of it. I don't think I ever saw a darker night.'

Shadow, the black horse, snorted noncommittal agreement and paced on.

'All right, if that's the way you feel about it,' Slade replied. 'Well, the wind's rising and should blow away some of the clouds soon, I figure. Then maybe we'll get a little moonshine to improve things. Anyhow, we shouldn't have much farther to go. That

1

ground traveling rainstorm over to your left is Corpus Christi Bay and the chances are we'll see the lights of the town before long. Hope so; the nosebag for you and a good surrounding for me won't go bad. Sort of short rations for both of us of late. So june along, horse, and keep your eyes skinned for moonlight or town light.'

However, neither appeared for the time being. The night remained utterly dark. Shadow's hoofbeats echoed back from the wall of chaparral flanking the trail on the right, the uneasy water gurgling and whimpering on the left, with the mist curtaining up from it.

Gradually, though, Slade became aware of a sparkle of light well out on the water and some distance ahead, a golden sparkle with a nimbus of saffroned mist around it.

Nothing unusual about that; there were plenty of ships on the bay. Looked like a riding light, for it appeared stationary. Slade wondered idly why a vessel should be anchored out there.

Shadow forged ahead, Slade slumped wearily in the saddle, half drowsing.

Abruptly he snapped wide awake. From somewhere out on the black water had come a scream, thin with distance, that crescendoed to a bubbling shriek and snapped off.

'Now what in blazes?' the Ranger wondered. He pulled Shadow to a halt to

2

listen better.

The sound was not repeated, but gradually he became aware of another and different sound, a rhythmic mutter that loudened to a thumping, the steady beat of oarlocks.

'Now what?' he exclaimed. 'Sure sounds like a rowboat is headed this way. Should hit the shore not far ahead. Slide along a little farther, horse.'

Shadow did so, but after a few paces Slade again halted him and sat listening to the loudening beat of the rowlocks. Now he could hear the splash of the oars.

'Sounds like a bunch of lubbers pulling them,' he muttered, 'they're catching crabs half the time.' He straightened in the saddle and peered ahead. He could see nothing, but to his ears had come still another alien sound, faint, musical but instantly identified by the acute hearing of El Halcón. The jingle of a bit iron as a horse tossed its head. Somewhere in the darkness a horse or horses were standing. What the devil was going on! He glanced up; the clouds were undoubtedly thinning as the strengthening wind beat upon them.

From the darkness ahead came a solid thump; the boat had grounded and from the racket it made he had a notion that the awkward oarsmen had run her aground hard, doubtless with her bow well up on the beach. A grumble of angry and disgusted oaths substantiated his surmise; somebody must have gotten a pretty hefty bump.

There was a mutter of words Slade could not catch, a creaking of saddle leather. He strained his eyes, futilely, but could only make out moving shadows in the faint light.

Then abruptly he had light aplenty, more than he wanted. The wind won its battle with the clouds; they rolled apart like a drawn curtain and moonlight streamed down, making the scene almost as bright as day.

The sudden transition was dazzling and it took a second or two for his eyes to focus properly.

Sitting horses, just as they were turning to the west, were half a dozen men. In that fleeting glimpse it seemed that five wore rangeland clothes, while the sixth did not. Then he had other things to think about. The horsemen sighted him as quickly as he did them. There were startled exclamations, a flashing of hands to holsters.

Slade went sideways from the saddle in a ripple of motion, whipping one of his guns from its sheath. A streak of orange flame gushed from the group; the slug fanned his face. His own Colt boomed and was echoed by a yelp of pain. He shot again. There was another yell. Bullets whined past, but the horsemen were shooting wildly and none found a mark. Prone on the ground, Slade fired again and again. A man coughed chokingly and slumped forward in his saddle.

As at a word of command, the group sent their horses scudding down the trail. Slade leaped to his feet, fired his last cartridge and slid his heavy Winchester from the saddle boot. But before he could line sights, the bunch whipped around a bend and out of sight.

Muttering wrathfully, El Halcón stood with the Winchester at the ready. But the hoofbeats did not cease and faded away in the distance. 'Now what the blankety-blank was that all about?' the Ranger growled as he sheathed the rifle, ejecting the spent shells from his Colt and replacing them with fresh cartridges.

His gaze centered on the boat that was driven well up on the beach. There was something huddled across one of the thwarts. With a last glance toward the bend, he strode to the boat and halted with an exclamation.

The thing huddled across the thwart was the body of a man. The haft of a heavy knife protruded from between his shoulder blades. Slade leaned close, staring.

The dead man wore what the rangeland called 'store clothes,' a neat business suit. His hat had fallen off to reveal grizzled hair. Slade was about to turn him over on his back for a look at his face. Instead, he straightened up, stood in an attitude of listening. A single bound and he was beside Shadow, forcing the black horse into the growth. Sure that he was concealed, he peered through the fringe of brush, listening to the drumming of fast hoofs coming from the east.

'We're not taking chances with anybody,' he breathed. 'Looks like any head that shows is fair game tonight. Quiet, feller, quiet!'

Shadow stood perfectly still, and Slade knew he was invisible from the trail.

Around the bend to the east bulged seven riders and eight horses, the last man of the bunch leading a saddled and bridled mount. As they drew abreast of where El Halcón and his horse stood motionless, a voice called out, 'There's the boat. Say, looks like the jigger is asleep. Guess he got tired of waiting and decided to take a snooze.'

Saddle leather popped, bits jingled as the group pulled to a halt.

'Henderson, wake up!' another voice called. Naturally there was no response from the stark occupant of the boat.

'Say, is the loco coot dead?' said the speaker as he swung from the saddle and approached the little craft. He took another step forward, halted as if struck. His voice rose in a horrified yell, 'For the love of Pete! he is dead! It's Henderson, and he's been knifed!'

A storm of voices arose, and a general dismounting. The whole bunch ran to the water's edge, staring, cursing, exclaiming.

'What in blazes does this mean?' demanded

6

the first speaker, a tall and broad-shouldered individual who Slade judged rightly was the leader of the bunch.

Nobody was able to answer. 'Must have been rowed from the ship by somebody,' one of the horsemen remarked. 'He couldn't have rowed that boat by himself.'

'And he hardly stuck that blade in his back himself,' the tall leader observed dryly. 'But where the devil did they go after doing for him?'

Apprehensive glances were cast about. Slade stood motion-less, hoping nobody would take a notion to investigate the chaparral. One round with nervous trigger fingers was enough for one night. For which reason he determined not to reveal himself to the group. No telling what their reaction might be.

'They must have had horses waiting here,' the leader said. 'Looks like somebody knew he was due to meet us here and got here first. I hate to touch him, but we've got to see if he's got the *dinero on* him.'

'Not likely to have,' one of the others said. 'Chances are that's what he was cashed in for.'

The leader entered the boat and turned the body over on its back. Slade wished he could get a glimpse of the dead face, but the men were grouped close around it, obscuring his view. Besides, thin patches of cloud kept drifting across the moon and the light was vague. The faces of the mysterious horsemen were just whitish blurs.

'Nope, nothing on him 'cept a few dollars I reckon were his,' said the leader. 'He'd hardly have been packing the money in his pockets. Must have had a gripsack or something, and it ain't here.'

'What we going to do with him?' somebody asked. The leader seemed to ponder a moment.

'Guess we'd better load him on the cayuse we brought for him to ride, and pack him to town and turn him over to the sheriff,' he decided.

'What if he blames us for what happened?'

'Not likely, with us packing the body in. And there's seven of us to tell the same story. No, we don't need to bother about Sheriff Davis. He hasn't much use for us, but he's a square man with plenty of savvy. He'll know we didn't do for poor Henderson. And we can't leave him here. Boat might wash away, or coyotes get to him. All right, haul him out and rope him to the saddle and let's head for town; getting late. Chances are we'll have to root the sheriff out of some rumhole as it is. That's right, Bill, you take his legs. I'll handle the other end. Let's go!'

The body was quickly roped into place. The group mounted and headed west at a brisk gait. Slade waited a few minutes, then drifted along behind them. With his unusually keen eyes he knew he could keep the moving

8

smudge which was his quarry in view without himself being spotted.

It really didn't matter if he lost sight of them, for there was little doubt but that they were headed for Corpus Christi and the sheriff's office, as the tall leader had said. He'd learn everything there was to learn when he arrived there.

'Well, if this hasn't been a loco night for fair,' he remarked to Shadow. 'First we hear a killing done. Then the apparent killers try to gun us. Next, along comes a bunch the murdered man was supposed to contact. Evidently he carried a large sum of money which the second bunch knew about. And it would appear the first bunch knew about it, too. As that tall jigger said, very likely that was what he was killed for. But why did he have a rendezvous with the second bunch at such an out-of-the-way meeting place? And to what use was the money he was packing to be put? Questions we haven't got the answer to, horse, but it's up to us to get the answers, and the answers to a few more. Out there on the bay lies Texas soil. Well, it looks like Captain Jim, as usual, knew what he was talking about when he 'lowed that some strange things were happening in this section and that we had better give the situation a once-over. June along, feller, I can still see them, and Corpus Christi can't be far off now.'

It wasn't. Another bend rounded and a

couple of miles ahead was a sparkle of lights that Slade knew must mark the two-tiered Bay town. He quickened Shadow's pace a little and he was no great distance behind the grim cavalcade when it reached the city's streets, where he lost track of them. Which didn't matter.

TWO

Acquainted with Corpus Christi, Slade knew where to find the office of the sheriff of Nueces County. He also knew that on an alley nearby was a livery stable that would provide suitable accommodations for Shadow. To the stable he made his way first.

It was still not very late and a light burned on the lower floor of the building. A knock on the door summoned the old keeper who held a bracket lamp, by the light of which he scrutinized his visitor. He peered with out-thrust neck, swore cheerfully.

'Well, well,' he exclaimed, 'so *you're* back! How are you, Mr. Slade? And how's the *caballo*? See! he remembers me. Bring him in, bring him in. The best in the house for him. He's some critter.'

'How are you, Sam?' Slade replied to the greeting. 'Yes, I'm back. Shadow insisted on me coming. Says there are no oats like

Sam's oats.'

The keeper chuckled and held out a gnarled hand, into which Shadow thrust his velvety muzzle and blew softly.

'A one-man horse, all right, but he doesn't forget his friends,' said Sam. He deftly stripped off the rig and led the big black to a stall.

'Got a place to sleep?' he asked Slade. 'No? The room next to mine, over the stalls, where you slept the last time you were here ain't got anybody in it tonight.'

'That'll be fine,' Slade accepted. 'I'll stow my rifle and my pouches while you're looking after the cayuse.'

'Key's in the door, and here's one to the front door,' said Sam. 'Try not to tear the place down when you come in drunk.'

'I'll do the best I can,' Slade promised gravely. He mounted the stairs, opened the door of the room designated, dropped his pouches and Winchester to the floor at the foot of the clean and comfortable looking bunk, closed and locked the door and descended.

Deciding it would be best to kill a bit of time before looking up Sheriff Davis, he sat down on an up-ended bucket and chatted with Sam for a while. After which he repaired to the sheriff's office and found, as he expected, the lank old frontiersman seated at his desk and looking anything but in a good temper as he glowered at a blanket-covered form on the floor.

The sheriff's eyes opened wide as his visitor entered, and he sat bolt upright.

'I might have known it! I might have known it!' he wailed. 'El Halcón and trouble! Or trouble and El Halcón! They go together like ham-and-eggs or horned toads and rattlesnakes! All right, all right, where are the rest of the carcasses, the ones *you* plugged?'

'Sorry to disappoint you, Berne, but really I wasn't mixed up in this deal at all,' Slade replied as they shook hands. 'I just happened to be in the nature of a witness to some of it.'

'Nacherly,' snorted the sheriff. 'You would be! All right, take a load off your feet and tell me what you saw.'

Slade sat down and rolled a cigarette with the fingers of his left hand before replying. He gestured to the blanket-covered body.

'First, just who and what was that poor devil?' he asked.

'Name's Henderson, Malcolm Henderson,' the sheriff answered. 'He is, or was, rather, a purchasing agent for the Westport Salvage and Shipping Company that has its headquarters here.'

Slade nodded. 'And who are the bunch that brought him in?'

Davis shot him a keen glance. 'So you know a bunch brought him in, eh?' he commented. 'That was Del Gregory and some of his Cross

G hellions,' he added, with a frown which did not escape Slade's attention.

'What's the matter with Gregory?' he asked abruptly. The sheriff hesitated.

'Oh, nothing for sure, except he's a trouble maker,' he replied.

'A cattleman?'

The sheriff nodded. 'Uh-huh, but he's run sheep onto his hill pastures, and that don't set over well with his neighbors.'

'Dick King ran forty thousand head on his big *Santa Gertrudis* ranch, not so far from here,' Slade pointed out.

'Uh-huh, but King owns all his land, plenty of it, and there's no danger of his darned woolies straying,' answered the sheriff. 'Over to the northeast is a lot of open range the cowmen use but don't own, and they're scared sheep will be run onto that. And you know what sheep can do to pasture.'

'If they're not handled properly,' Slade agreed. 'Handled as they should be, there is no reason why sheep and cows can't get along in the same section, to the benefit of both. It's being done in other parts of Texas, and sooner or later it'll be done here despite the protests of the cowmen who will eventually realize that sheep on their hill pastures that are not good for cows will tide them over bad spells.'

The sheriff nodded, but, an old cowman himself, didn't look convinced.

'But getting back to Henderson,' Slade

resumed. 'What did Gregory and his bunch tell you about him?'

'Nothing much,' replied Davis. 'They said they found him lying in a boat beached about four miles to the east of here, with that knife stuck in his back, and figured they'd better pack him in to me. Guess they didn't have anything to do with the killing, but I can't help wondering a mite; they're a salty bunch.'

'They didn't have,' Slade said. 'I'll tell you what I know about the matter.'

He proceeded to do so, refraining, however, from mentioning the fact that Gregory and his men undoubtedly knew Henderson and had an appointment with him, an appointment that apparently had to do with a large sum of money the purchasing agent was supposed to be packing. That being an angle he preferred to keep to himself, at least for the time being, and which set him to do some serious thinking about Del Gregory and his riders. One thought kept hammering in his brain: if it was a legitimate deal they had in mind, why didn't they tell the sheriff about it?

Of course there was one possible explanation. Gregory had remarked that the sheriff didn't have much use for him and his bunch. So because of the sheriff's attitude he had been reluctant to discuss matters with him.

In fact, the whole affair smacked of

14

something not just exactly above board. Why had the purchasing agent of the salvage and shipping company chosen to meet the Cross G representatives at such a place, under such circumstances and at such a time?

Those questions and others must be answered to the Ranger's satisfaction, who had been to a certain extent a 'witness' to a murder committed within the territorial limits of Texas. That it was a murder and not an accidental killing or a killing in hot blood was obvious.

'What I'd like to know is who the devil were the hellions who brought Henderson's body to shore,' remarked the sheriff. 'You say they were dressed as cowhands?'

'Five of them were,' Slade replied. 'The other, so far as I could judge, wore the garb usually associated with deckhands. Not that either necessarily means much. Plenty of gents wearing rangeland clothes are not and haven't been for quite a spell cowhands. The same of someone dressed as a deckhand. Things were a mite hectic right then, but it appeared to me that all six forked their horses in rangeland style. Anyhow, if you hear of any gents coming to the doctor to get patched up, keep an eye on them. I'm pretty sure I nicked a couple. Not seriously enough to drop them from their hulls, though. They all kept going. I didn't think it wise to try and catch them up.'

'Would have been plain darned foolishness

to try,' grunted the sheriff. 'Nacherly, too, you wanted a look at what was in the boat.'

'Yes, but I didn't get much of a look,' Slade nodded. 'Before I could even turn him over on his back I heard the other bunch coming and figured I'd better make myself scarce.'

'That was smart, too,' said Davis. 'Those Cross G hellions have itchy trigger fingers.' Slade nodded and sat, pondering a moment.

'What about the outfit Henderson worked for, the Westport Salvage and Shipping Company I believe you said.'

The sheriff shrugged. 'Okay, so far as I've been able to ascertain,' he replied. 'Set up in business here about a year back. We've got two of 'em here—the Westport and the Aransas, which hasn't been here quite so long. I wouldn't put it past either of them to cut a corner a mite now and then, always that way with competitive businesses. They find plenty to do. Go in for coastwise trading and salvage operations of one sort or another. Old tubs are always getting into trouble out on the bay or the Gulf and needing tows or repair jobs.'

'And each tries to grab the business,' Slade commented.

'That's right,' conceded the sheriff. 'Plenty of rivalry between them, sometimes almost amounting to bad blood, I'd say. Some of their crews have started a ruckus or two of late, when those representing the outfits happened to get together.'

16

'That's interesting,' Slade commented.

'Uh-huh,' said Davis, 'but I don't pay those ruckuses much mind. Let the town marshal and his coupla flatfoots take care of 'em. I've got real troubles on my hands.'

'Getting back to the bunch that brought in Henderson's body,' Slade said. 'I've a notion the one dressed as a deckhand or sailor was neither.'

'How do you figure that?' asked Davis.

'I listened to that boat come to shore,' Slade explained. 'If the fellow was a sailor it is logical to assume that he would have been handling one of the oars. Either he wasn't or he was no real sailor. Whoever pulled those oars was certainly not experienced at the chore. Their strokes were very choppy, the sort expected from a landlubber.'

'Smart reasoning,' the sheriff said admiringly. ' 'Bout what would be expected from El Halcón, though. I suppose you're hanging onto that loco monicker, eh?'

'That's right,' Slade replied. 'There are only a few folks hereabouts who know I'm a Ranger, and they will keep their mouths shut.'

'And some trigger-happy marshal or deputy is liable to shut *your* mouth for good because of that darn foolishness, to say nothing of a gun-slinger out to get a reputation by downing the notorious El Halcón, and not above shooting in the back to do it,' growled Davis.

Slade smiled. But he knew there was truth

17

in what the sheriff said.

Due to his habit of working under cover whenever possible and often not revealing his Ranger connections, Walt Slade had built up a peculiar dual reputation. Those who knew the truth were wont to declare that he was the ablest as well as the most fearless of the illustrious body of law enforcement officers. Those who didn't opined that he was just a blasted owlhoot too smart to get caught, so far, but who would slip sooner or later and get his comeuppance.

This worried Captain Jim McNelty, the famous Commander of the Border Battalion of the Texas Rangers, and he often remonstrated with his Lieutenant and ace man for fostering the deception. But Slade pointed out that as El Halcón of dubious reputation, avenues of information were open to him that would be closed to a known Ranger. Also, outlaws, thinking him to be one of their own brand, were likely to grow careless and take chances.

So Captain Jim would grumble and shake his grizzled head but not actually command Slade to desist. While Slade went his careless way as El Halcón, the 'singingest man in the whole Southwest with the fastest gunhand,' and worried not at all.

THREE

Davis glanced at the body on the floor. 'We'll be holding an inquest on him tomorrow,' he observed. 'I suppose you want to keep out of it?'

'I'd prefer it that way,' Slade replied. 'Really there's not much I could give that would be of value to the coroner's jury. I didn't see him killed, and although I got a glimpse of those I suppose were responsible for his death, I couldn't identify any of them and I couldn't even swear that they had anything to do with his death; would just be conjecture on my part, and conjecture carries no weight in a court of law. Better that the hellions who brought him ashore and who undoubtedly *were* responsible for his death don't know that I witnessed their actions. Thinking they were perfectly in the clear might cause them to grow careless.'

'Uh-huh, and there's another angle to consider, though being what you are, I suppose you wouldn't pay it any mind. If you testified to what you say, while you don't know who they are, they'd know who you are and would have you at a disadvantage.'

'Truth in that, all right,' Slade conceded. 'And perhaps I pay it more mind than you think.' Davis grunted and didn't look convinced.

'Now what?' he asked.

Slade sat thinking for a few moments before replying. Davis, who respected El Halcón's silences, did not interrupt but watched him expectantly.

What a splendid looking man he was, thought the sheriff. Very tall, more than six feet, with broad shoulders and hands that were strong as woven steel.

His face was as arresting as his form. Lean, deeply bronzed, a rather wide mouth, grin-quirked at the corners, which relieved somewhat the tinge of fierceness evinced by the prominent hawk nose above and the powerful jaw and chin beneath. His hair was black, and thick.

The sternly handsome countenance was dominated by blacklashed eyes of very pale gray. Cold, reckless eyes that nevertheless always seemed to have little devils of laughter lurking in their clear depths. Devils that could leap to the front in kindliness and mirth or could, under certain circumstances, change to devils of a very different sort and devoid of laughter.

Slade wore the homely but efficient garb of the rangeland, and wore it with the careless grace with which Richard the Lion Hearted must have worn armor. His Levis, the bibless overalls favored by the cowhand, were tucked into high-heeled half-boots of softly tanned leather. A faded blue shirt with vivid handkerchief looped at the throat and a well-worn 'J.B.' completed his costume.

Circling his sinewy waist were double cartridge belts, from which protruded the plain black butts of heavy guns in their carefully worked and oiled cut-out holsters. And from the butts of those guns his hands seemed never far away.

Slade broke the silence. 'I'd like to get a look at Gregory and his bunch,' he said. 'First, though, I hanker for thing to eat. Been quite a while since breakfast, and not much of a breakfast at that.'

'Fine,' said the sheriff, rising to his feet. 'I'm hungry, too. And maybe we can knock over a couple of gophers with the same rock. I know where Gregory and his hands usually hang out when they're in town. A rumhole down on Water Street, sorta rough, and they do put out a surrounding of good chuck. Called the Matagorda, and a sorta good name for it. Old Matagorda Bay is famous for storms kicking up all of a sudden, and so's the rumhole. Peaceful and quiet one minute, blows sky high the next. Cowhands go there, and seamen, and others the less said about the better.'

'Sounds plumb interesting,' Slade smiled.

'Too darn interesting at times,' grunted the sheriff. 'Never can tell when the roof's going to fall in on you. That goes for quite a few of the joints down by the bay. Let's go.'

It wasn't a very long walk to Water Street and they reached the Matagorda without incident. Fronting the saloon was a long hitchrack, at which a number of cow ponies were tethered. Sheriff Davis peered at the brands.

'Yep, they're in there,' he announced. 'That chestnut has a Cross G burn and so has the dun next to it.'

They pushed their way through the swinging door, over which came strains of music and a babble of voices. Glancing about, Slade didn't think the place looked too bad. It was large, fairly well lighted by a big hanging lamp over the bar, another over the dance-floor. The bar was long, spanning one whole end of the room. There were a couple of roulette wheels, both spinning, a faro bank, poker tables, also doing business. The orchestra was not bad, Slade thought, and the girls on the dance-floor weren't too bad, either. There was a lunch counter, and tables for patrons who preferred more leisurely eating. The room was pretty well crowded and the gathering was a varied one. Cowhands, of which there were a number, stood shoulder to shoulder with gents who were evidently seamen, of whom there was even a larger number. Well-dressed individuals wearing store clothes chatted together. These, the Ranger decided, were very likely shopkeepers or workers in the various establishments that lined the waterfront. And there were gentlemen in rangeland dress who looked to be cowhands but probably hadn't been for quite a while, whose antecedents were doubtless dubious, their presents questionable, their futures unpredictable. These last interested El Halcón.

A smiling waiter came forward to meet them, called the sheriff by name and led them to a table near the dance-floor. Slade and Davis gave their order, the former rolled a cigarette, the sheriff hauled out a black pipe and stuffed it with blacker tobacco.

'See the bunch hanging together over toward the end of the bar?' he said. 'The big feller is Del Gregory. The others are his hands.'

Slade surveyed with interest the bunch that brought in Henderson's body. Gregory was outstanding. He was tall, well formed, with flashing dark eyes and a bronzed face. In contrast to his dark eyes, his hair was a very light brown verging on yellow. He had a tight mouth, a straight nose and prominent chin. Altogether not a bad looking jigger except for a certain expression of arrogance. Had a temper that wasn't always under control, Slade deduced. His companions were average-appearing cowhands with nothing to distinguish them from others of their kind. A jovial-looking bunch that could under provocation very likely be plenty salty.

Next to the Cross G rannies, but seeming to edge away from them, was another bunch of waddies of about the same number. Doubtless all belonging to the same outfit, Slade decided, for they talked together in low tones over their drinks, of which they were downing plenty.

All in all, Slade felt that Sheriff Davis' remarks comparing the saloon to its namesake, Matagorda Bay, were not out of order. The place was peaceful enough at the moment but was potentially explosive.

Their dinner arrived and both went to work on it, during which conversation languished. Finally the sheriff pushed back his empty plate with a sigh of satisfaction.

'Think I'll have a snort to hold the chuck down,' he decided. 'How about you?'

'I believe I'll settle for another cup of coffee at the moment,' Slade replied.

The coffee and the snort were brought and the two peace officers, full fed and content, settled back to smoke the pipe, and cigarette, of peace and well being.

However, the peace was not of the enduring brand. Standing closest to the Cross G bunch was a heavy-set cowhand with a blocky, irascible-looking face. Suddenly Del Gregory whirled and sent him reeling with the flat of a hand across his mouth. Instantly the whole end of the bar was a hitting, kicking, gouging, wrestling tussle as the two outfits tangled.

Sheriff Davis started up from his chair, but Slade laid a restraining hand on his arm.

'Take it easy,' he advised. 'It's just a fist wring and won't amount to much.'

It didn't amount to much. The owner, a husky gent with a handlebar mustache, two equally husky floor men, and several waiters shouldered between the combatants and hurled them apart. They drew back, glowering sullenly. A bartender waved a sawed-off shotgun in a persuasive manner, called for order, and got it. The two groups returned to their drinks, nursing sundry bruises and a bloody nose or two.

'Now what the devil started that?' wondered the sheriff.

'Didn't you hear?' Slade asked.

'I ain't got El Halcón's ears,' Davis snorted. 'All I heard was the smack of Gregory's hand when he larruped Tobe Larsen.'

'Well, the jigger you call Larsen said, "Smells mighty strong of sheep in here." Gregory evidently didn't like it.'

'Reckon he didn't,' growled the sheriff. 'Darn sheep, anyhow! They always cause trouble.'

Slade chuckled and drank some coffee.

'Who is Larsen and his bunch?' he asked.

'Some of Watson Payne's Circle P hands,' the sheriff answered. 'Payne owns a spread over to the west. Newcomer; been here about a year. They're usually a pretty well-behaved bunch. But like most cowmen, they don't go for sheep.'

'They'll do well to be a little less vocal in their dislike,' Slade observed dryly. 'A loose *látigo* on one's jaw is often productive of trouble.'

'As I reckon Larsen realizes right now,' conceded Davis. 'Just the same I don't like it. A row like that between two outfits can build up to something big; it's happened before.'

Slade nodded sober agreement. It had, and could again.

The age-old conflict between 'Bossy' and 'Mary's Little Lamb!' Even in the Old Testament are accounts of sheep versus cattle rows,

> 'Woe be to the shepherds of
> Israel . . . Seemeth it a small
> thing unto you to have eaten up
> the good pasture, but ye must tread
>   down with
> your feet the residue of your pasture? . . .

And:

> 'For every shepherd is an
> abomination unto the Egyptians.'

Improperly handled, sheep do destroy range. They eat the land bare when grass is

26

scant, cropping it down to the ground and, with their chisel feet driven by a hundred pounds of solid bone and flesh, cut even the roots of the grass to powder, leaving barren ground that will not hold moisture.

However, Slade did not believe that a serious range war would result in this section because of the encroachment of sheep. More and more cowmen were realizing it was futile to fight sheep, and were concentrating on the proper handling of them. Keep the woolies on the move and they do no damage.

Of course there would be individual rows such as the one he had just witnessed, but he did not think it would go much beyond that. Of course, he knew, he could be wrong, which would unpleasantly complicate things and give him another problem to face in addition to the mysterious killings, robberies, and ship wreckings he had been sent to investigate.

Well, all he could do was hope for the best and be prepared for worst, as the saying went.

Surveying the groups at the bar, Slade noticed that Del Gregory had a handkerchief wrapped around his right hand, which plainly showed a blood stain; looked like he had cut his hand in the course of the scuffle.

A little later the Circle P hands, with compressed lips and clouded brows, filed out, casting menacing glances at their erstwhile opponents but making no untoward move. After a moment or two, Del Gregory sauntered over to the table.

'I'm sorry for what happened, Berne,' he said. 'I shouldn't have lost my temper that way, but Larsen got me riled.'

'You're always going off half-cocked,' growled the sheriff. 'You've got the disposition of a teased snake.'

Gregory grinned, showing crooked teeth that were as white as Slade's.

'Guess you're right,' he conceded. 'Just made that way, I reckon.'

'Well, try and do a little chore of unmaking,' grunted Davis. 'Get along better with folks if you do.' Gregory grinned again but did not argue. Slade addressed the ranch owner.

'Mr. Gregory,' he said, 'let me have a look at that hand of yours. Appears to be bleeding rather profusely.'

Gregory shot him a glance, then undid the bloody handkerchief.

'Just a scratch,' he said. 'Cut it on one of Larsen's teeth when I walloped him.'

Slade examined the deep cut in the palm. 'It is more than a scratch,' he said. 'You should see a doctor without delay. A cut from a human tooth can develop into something serious. You may have a very sore hand if it is not attended to, with the chance of losing it.'

Gregory looked startled. Sheriff Davis spoke, 'Better do what Slade tells you, Del. Always a good notion to do what he says.'

Gregory shot El Halcón another glance, speculative this time.

'Yes,' he said slowly, 'I've a notion it is.'

Davis stood up. 'I'll go with you to rout out Doc Cooper,' he said. 'Don't mind waiting, do you, Walt? Be back in a jiffy.'

'Go ahead,' Slade replied. 'I'll be right here when you get back.'

Gregory paused at the bar to say a word to his men, then he and the sheriff left the saloon. Slade settled back comfortably with his coffee and cigarette; then abruptly he sat bolt upright.

From outside the saloon had come the muffled boom of a gun. Almost instantly the report was followed by a crackling volley.

FOUR

Although he was seated on the far side of the room, Slade was the first man to reach the sidewalk. He had crossed the room with panther-like bounds before the other startled occupants made a move. Reaching the outside, hands close to his guns, he glanced left and right.

Here the street was dimly lighted. Less than a dozen paces to his left was the black mouth of a narrow alley. Facing the alley, gun in hand, was the lanky form of Sheriff Davis. On the sidewalk at his feet lay the motionless body of a man. The sheriff turned as Slade raced to his side.

'What happened?' the Ranger asked.

'Hellion took a shot at us from the alley,' replied Davis, glaring into its dark mouth. 'I cut down on him but I'm scairt he got in the clear. 'Fraid he did for poor Gregory.'

Slade glanced up the alley but could see no signs of movement there. No sound came from its gloomy depths.

'Watch it,' he told the sheriff and knelt beside Gregory.

A quick glance told him the cattleman was not dead. His chest rose and fell spasmodically. Along the side of his head, just below the forehead hairline, was a long gash that was bleeding freely. Slade probed the area of the wound with sensitive fingers.

'Just creased,' he told the sheriff. 'He'll be coming out of it soon. Hit him a hard lick, though. An inch to the left and he would be a goner. I'll get to work on him as soon as he rouses up.'

Gregory was indeed grunting and muttering with returning consciousness, and rolling his bloody head from side to side.

'Keep the crowd back, Berne,' Slade snapped. Another moment and Gregory's eyes opened. He stared wildly, mumbled and muttered.

'Take it easy,' Slade told him.

With Slade's arm around his shoulder he achieved a sitting position, groaned and held his head in his hands.

'Stay right as you are,' Slade said. He drew a clean handkerchief from his pocket, and deftly formed a pad which he applied to the wound to check the bleeding. With his neckkerchief he bound it securely in place. Then he rolled a cigarette, lit it and placed. it between the rancher's lips. Gregory took a couple of deep drags.

'That helped,' he said, his voice natural again.

The Cross G hands had shouldered their way to the front.

'Boss, you all right?' one, who Slade later learned was Alf Livesay, the Cross G range boss, asked anxiously.

'All right, 'cept for a blankety-blank headache,' Gregory replied. 'Was close, though.'

Livesay, big, bulky and hard looking, let out a string of curses.

'Those blankety-blank snake-blooded Circle P hellions!' he swore. 'Drygulchin' a man from an alley! All right, boys, we'll run the side-winders down and make a cleaning of that nest of varmints.'

Walt Slade straightened up. 'You'll do nothing of the kind,' he said, his eyes boring into Livesay's. 'You have no proof that the Circle P outfit had anything to do with this.

You're staying right here. Do you understand?'

Under the threat in El Halcón's icy eyes, Livesay subsided to muttered oaths and made no move. Later, he told Del Gregory, 'It was his blasted eyes that did it. Never saw such eyes. They went through me like a greased knife, and took all the fight out of me. I figured I'd better do as he said, and I think I figured right.'

Slade returned to Gregory. 'Think you can stand?' he asked. 'Okay, I'll give you a lift. There! Hold onto him for just a minute, Berne. Then we'll take him to the doctor. Guess we'd better hustle before he collects some more punctures; this just isn't his night.'

Gregory chuckled feebly and leaned on the sheriff's armn. Slade turned and entered the alley with quick, light steps and explored it to its far mouth, and found nothing.

'The devil made it out,' he told Davis when he returned. 'Guess you didn't connect with him.'

'There wasn't a darn thing to shoot at in the dark,' the sheriff replied. 'I just cut loose on general principle. Grabbed hold of Del and tried to keep him from falling first. That gave the horned toad a start.'

Slade nodded. 'All right, let's go,' he said.

'Can I come back here after Doc finishes with me?' Gregory asked Slade.

'Unless he orders otherwise,' the Ranger answered. Gregory turned to his hands.

32

'You heard, boys. Wait for me here.'

'If the doctor decides to hold him, I'll come and tell you,' Slade added.

'Much obliged, feller,' said Alf Livesay. 'You're a right *hombre*, if you don't mind me saying so.'

Slade smiled at him, the flashing white smile of El Halcón that men and women found irresistible.

'Thank you for saying it,' he replied. Livesay grinned sheepishly, fumbled with his hands and looked embarrassed.

'I don't know who he is or what he is, but I meant just what I said,' he remarked to his men as Gregory, with Slade and the sheriff supporting him, moved off.

'And you're purty good at sizing folks up right, Alf,' one of the punchers observed. 'Say! did you notice how he took charge of things right off and how everybody, including Berne Davis, did just exactly what he told them to without arg'fying.'

'I've a notion it would have been darn unhealthy to do otherwise,' Livesay commented dryly. 'Let's go get a drink.'

The shock he had suffered from the rap on his skull wearing off, Gregory quickly picked up strength and it didn't take them long to reach the doctor's office. Repeated hammering brought the old frontier practitioner to the door, clad in slippers and a long nightshirt and holding a lighted lamp aloft. Grumbling profanity, he peered at his visitors, his gaze settled on Slade's face and his left eyelid flickered in a barely perceptible wink.

'All right, all right, what in blazes?' he demanded. 'Oh, it's you, Gregory. Been in another shindig, eh? Bring him in and set him in that chair till I get my pants on. How are you, Berne? Who's your high-pockets *amigo?*'

Davis performed the introductions. Slade and Cooper, who knew each other well, shook hands solemnly, their faces devoid of expression. Doc ambled into his bedroom and came out a moment later more fully garbed. Without delay he went to work on Gregory.

To the bullet slice he paid scant attention, merely replacing Slade's pad and bandage with clean ones.

'You retarded the bleeding properly and that was all it needed,' he told El Halcón. 'Nothing to it.'

'I could find no indications of fracture or concussion,' the Ranger observed.

'And if you couldn't, nobody else could,' Doc grunted. 'Surgeon's hands if I ever saw a pair. This cut on his hand is something else, though. Got it from the teeth of the jigger you walloped, eh? Without proper care that could lead to serious results.'

'So Slade told me,' Gregory put in.

'Slade was right,' said the doctor. 'If a dog or a wolf fangs you, throw some water on the

34

cut and you're okay, but if a man bites you, look out! The human mouth is a hotbed of disease. All kinds of germs all the time holding a grand reunion there.'

He cleansed and cauterized the wound, applied antiseptic ointment and a bandage.

'If it starts swelling, you get to me pronto,' he warned the rancher.

'I'll do that,' Gregory promised. He shot Slade a grateful glance.

'And if it hadn't been for you,' he told the Ranger, 'I might have ended up short a paw. I wouldn't have paid the darn thing any mind.'

'You'd have paid it mind if it had started puffing and pains and red streaks shooting up your arm,' the doctor growled. 'All right, that's all for now, and I crave shuteye.'

Gregory pressed a bill into his gnarled old hand. Doc glanced at the denomination.

'That's twice my fee,' he protested.

'And if you don't take it, I'll feel twice as bad as I do now,' Gregory retorted. *'Buenos noches!'*

When they reached the street, Slade said, 'Well walk back to the saloon with you. I feel the need of a snort about now.'

His real objective was further opportunity to study Gregory and his hands, for he had not yet made up his mind concerning the Cross G owner and his bunch.

When they reached the saloon, Gregory insisted on buying the drinks. Slade finished his and announced, 'I'm going to bed; beginning to feel a mite weary.'

'Me, too,' the sheriff agreed. 'Be seeing you, Del.'

'Ride over to my place when you get a chance, I'd like to have a talk with you,' Gregory invited Slade. 'About seven miles to the east of here. Old white ranchhouse in a grove of burr oaks. Can't miss it, left of the trail. Bay's on the right. Yes, well be here tomorrow for the inquest, Berne. Not much we can tell, though.'

Outside the saloon, Davis said to Slade, 'Well, what do you think of it?'

'I think,' Slade replied, 'that those hellions who brought Henderson's body ashore got a better look at me than I'd figured they did.'

Davis gave him a startled glance. 'Now what the devil do you mean by that?' he demanded.

'I mean,' Slade answered, 'that, in my opinion, Del Gregory was the victim of mistaken identity.'

'The devil you say! How do you figure it?'

'In the first place,' Slade explained, 'the lighting down here is very poor; be difficult for a man in the alley mouth to distinguish the features of anyone walking along the street. Gregory is not quite as tall as myself, but he's not far from it, and he's about as broad. Next, you and I entered the Matagorda together. Would be logical to assume that we would leave together, and that we would walk past

36

that alley on our way uptown, whereas Gregory would undoubtedly leave with his hands in attendance. They would not walk east along the street but would go to their horses, which are tethered this side of the alley. They would have no reason for passing the alley.'

Sheriff Davis cast a nervous glance at the alley in question, which was but a few yards distant.

'Let's get out of here,' he suggested. 'You can tell me the rest of it while we're walking.'

'I don't think there's much danger of another try tonight,' Slade observed as they moved on.

The sheriff nodded, but his hand was on his gun butt and his eyes probed the alley as they passed; he walked with his chin on his shoulder until they were some distance beyond the sinister lane.

'All right, what else?' he asked as he faced to the front again.

'Out there on the trail where the boat was beached, the moon shone full on my face, while theirs were practically in the shadow,' Slade resumed. 'I didn't get anything like a good look at any of them. However, they wouldn't have known that for sure and perhaps figured I did get a good enough look at them to be able to recognize them if I saw them again.'

'And didn't want any witnesses to their

skullduggery hanging around, eh?'

'Exactly.'

'Puts you on a nice spot,' Davis growled. 'They know who to look for and you don't.'

'Chances are they'll give themselves away, if I happen to run into them,' Slade replied cheerfully.

Although he did not really anticipate another attack, Slade approached the livery stable warily, surveying his surroundings with care, listening for any untoward sound as he unlocked and opened the door. Everything was peaceful and he reached his room without incident. The building vibrated to old Sam's snores but otherwise no sound broke the somnolent silence. After cleaning and oiling his guns he tumbled into bed, and slept soundly until almost noon.

FIVE

When Slade awoke, with brilliant sunshine streaming through the window, he did not immediately get up but lay for a while pondering the turbulent incidents of the past twenty-four hours.

They had been plenty turbulent, all right. The big question, of course, was who killed Malcolm Henderson, the salvage company's purchasing—agent. Presumably with robbery the motive. Dove-tailing with that was another interrogation: how was it that Henderson trusted himself in the boat with his killers when he had an appointment with another group? Intertwined, Slade felt, was the real motive back of the killing, in relation to which the stealing of the money Henderson was supposed to carry might be but incidental.

And for what purpose was his anticipated contact with Del Gregory and his bunch? And why was the Cross G owner so close-mouthed about the proposed meeting, refraining from mentioning it to the sheriff as he did?

Of course that might permit of a legitimate explanation. A deal, perhaps; it was thought wise to keep a secret from a competitor. But who was the competitor?

Around and around, and getting exactly nowhere. Well, Captain Jim had said that the section had been plagued of late by several mysterious killings and a couple of ships wrecked under what appeared to be suspicious circumstances; his reason for dispatching his ace man to investigate. Looked like the recent happenings tied in very neatly with former ones. Well, maybe things would work out; they always seemed to. Slade arose hungry and in a peaceful frame of mind.

A sluice in the icy waters of the big trough in the back of the stable helped, as did a shave. Bestowing a pat on Shadow and saying so long to Sam, he sallied forth in search of some breakfast.

Obeying a sudden impulse, he made his way to the Matagorda saloon; the chuck there had proved okay and he wanted to get a look at the place and its patrons by daylight. He had a feeling that the dubious activities might well focus there.

The waterfront was quite different from its gloom and silence of the night before. Everywhere was a cheerful and bustling activity. Several battered and dissolute steamers were moored at the wharf, and a trim three-masted brig.

Also three very capable-looking big tugs. Two of these bore the legend, Westport Salvage and Shipping Company. The other, Aransas Salvage and Shipping. Owned, evidently, by the companies Sheriff Davis mentioned. Slade wondered if either of the first two had been the vessel moored off-shore the previous evening, from which Malcolm Henderson had set to for his rendezvous with death. Perhaps something relative to that would come to light at the inquest which would be held within the next two hours.

The Matagorda also looked better with the sunlight streaming through its windows to make glowing patterns on the floor and walls. The patrons at the moment, Slade noted, were nearly all seamen, with a sprinkling of storeclothes individuals. There were no cowhands present.

He found a table and gave his order to a cheerful and corpulent waiter who looked as if he sampled bountifully of the Matagorda's culinary efforts and thrived thereby. A good advertisement for the place.

Slade enjoyed an excellent breakfast, then lingered over a cigarette and a final cup of coffee. His thoughts turned to Del Gregory and his hands, and the puzzling question. What was the contemplated deal in which the murdered Henderson had been mixed up? They seemed all right, not the sort to go in for shady practices, but you never could tell. He knew that just as there is no such thing as a criminal physiognomy, neither is there a precise pattern of operations relegated to the criminally inclined. Outlaws could be, and sometimes were, the most jovial and congenial individuals who in their off moments were no different from their law abiding fellows. Could be the case with Del Gregory and his bunch. Well, he'd just have to await developments and keep his eyes open. He pinched out his cigarette, paid his score and left the saloon.

It was still some time until the inquest would be held so he decided to loaf around the waterfront for a while. His gaze rested idly on the three tugs that represented the rival salvage and shipping companies, and as he gazed he observed a small steam launch scudding in from the outer bay. A little later, she slid alongside one of the Westport tugs, over the rail of which men were leaning. Men were also leaning over the rail of the nearby Aransas tug.

A man stood up in the launch, shouted something Slade did not catch. Instantly the tug's deck was a scene of activity. At the same moment, the Aransas' tug's funnel belched black smoke to the roar of a forced draught. She swung around, 'on a dime,' and bellowed away from the wharf, heading west.

From the Westport's deck went up a volley of profanity. Fists were shaken at the Aransas. Her stack also began to boom, but it seemed she didn't have steam up. In a very few minutes, however, she too went charging out of the harbor, in the wake of the Aransas.

Slade heard a chuckle at his elbow and turned to face a weatherbeaten old salt who had strolled up beside him, his gaze fixed on the Aransas tug now growing small against the waves.

'What is it, a race?' he asked. The sailor chuckled again.

'Sort of,' he replied. 'That launch brought word there's a steamer stuck on a reef over to the west of here and needs to be hauled clear. The swab that's first to lay a line on her will get good money for the job.

'Yep, big money,' he repeated, 'but where those swabs really make a haul is when they sight a ship that's been abandoned and haul her to port. Then they can claim just about what they please, and get it.'

Slade nodded. He knew that the United States district courts often awarded a very high percentage of the value of ship and cargo to a salvage crew. Highest when the vessel in question appeared to be a derelict, abandoned by a crew with no intention of returning.

'The Aransas got two of that sort and the Westport one in the past six months,' the loquacious sailor continued. 'The Westport's was an old tramp loading hides and tallow and wasn't worth so much, but the two the Aransas dropped lines on were laden with mighty valuable cargo, I heard.'

'Why were they abandoned?' Slade asked. The oldster shrugged.

'Hard to tell,' he equivocated. 'Never know what those coastwise lubbers will do. They're a worthless lot,' he added, with the true deep-water man's contempt for the 'shorebound' sailors who plied the bays, the river and the Gulf coast and never got far out of sight of land.

'Liable to be a row between those two over this,' the sailor continued. 'For some reason, the launch brought the word to the Westport, but the Aransas heard it too, and having steam up sorta got the jump on the Westport. Yep, liable to be a row. The Westporters will feel they should have first try at warping her off that reef. Won't do 'em any good, though, 'cept for the fun of bustin' a nose or two, if

43

they ain't first to lay a line across her. In a case like this, first lubber to the galley gets the first whack of lobscouse. Hey! there goes the other Westport tug; reckon they want to get in on the shindig. Wish I was over there; should be worth watching if they do run afoul of each other.'

'The chances are it would be,' Slade agreed, and meant it. Such crews were not noted for sweetness and light and there would very likely be a lively wring before the affair was finished. Well, there was nothing he could do about it. He said goodbye to the old sailor and strolled on, heading for the sheriff's office.

When he arrived there he found Davis had company, a big, powerfully built man with grizzled hair. He had a well-featured face, a firm mouth and light blue eyes.

'Hi, Walt,' the sheriff greeted. 'Want you and Watson Payne to know each other, Slade. Watson owns the Circle P spread over to the west of here. You saw some of his hands last night. Sorta own the Aransas Company, too, eh, Watson?'

'Well, I guess I'm the largest stockholder,' Payne admitted with a pleasant smile as he shook hands, his grip firm but not obtrusively so. 'New to the section, Mr. Slade?'

'I am not a resident of Nueces County, but I've visited Corpus Christi a couple of times before,' Slade replied.

'Good section to coil your twine in,' said

Payne. 'Up and coming. This town is going to go places or I'm a lot mistaken. I figure I made a wise move by moving here.'

'Walt's a particular friend of mine,' the sheriff observed.

'There could be no better recommendation,' Payne declared heartily. 'Well, Berne, I guess it's about time for the inquest to be held, is it not? I'm anxious to hear what's said.' He turned to Slade.

'The Westport people and my outfit are business rivals, but we never carry our feuds past the office door,' he said. 'I was deeply shocked when I heard what happened to poor Henderson. He always struck me as being a very pleasant person. I can't for the life of me understand it. What in the world was he doing out there in a rowboat? The whole affair just doesn't seem to make sense.'

'It certainly doesn't,' Slade agreed soberly. So far as that particular angle went, he and Watson Payne were in accord.

'Nobody can understand it any more than we can understand the other blankety-blank things that have been happening hereabouts of late,' growled the sheriff. 'All right, let's go. Doc Cooper, the coroner, will be banging his gavel any minute now. If we barge in making a noise after proceedings start he's liable to throw us all in the calaboose for contempt of court; he's a cantankerous old coot.'

The inquest was brief, and productive of no

45

tangible results. Slade listened closely to the testimony given by Del Gregory and his hands. So far as he was able to judge, it differed not at all from the story they told the sheriff when they brought in Henderson's body.

Which impressed El Halcón. People who have but one story to tell seldom vary it no matter how many times it is repeated, especially if it happens to be true.

The coroner's jury 'lowed that Malcolm Henderson met his death at the hands of a party or parties unknown and advised Sheriff Davis to rattle his hocks and bring in the hellion as quickly as possible. An admonition that did not appear to set well with that peace officer.

'Getting darned monotonous,' he growled to Slade. 'I've been hearing the same thing over and over for the past six months.'

Watson Payne shook hands again with Slade before taking his departure.

'Drop in and see me if you happen to ride over to the west,' he invited. 'You'll be very welcome.'

Sheriff Davis speculated his departing form. 'A nice feller,' he commented. 'Knows the cow business, too. Has had plenty of experience in the shipping business, too. He took over the Company when it was an old outfit over at Galveston, then moved it here. He's all right.'

'Appears to be,' Slade conceded.

'Now what?' Davis asked.

'Now, if it is plausible, I'd like to meet the head of the Westport Company,' Slade replied.

For some reason, the request caused the sheriff to chuckle, but all he said was, 'Okay, I think I can fix it. Their office is just a few blocks away, on Mesquite Street. Let's go.'

Shortly they arrived at the building which housed the salvage company's office. When they entered, an elderly and cheerful looking individual working at a desk nodded a greeting.

'Boss in, Mack?' the sheriff asked. The other gestured to a half open door. 'Yep,' he said.

'Come right in, Sheriff,' a feminine voice, a very nice voice, called.

Davis pushed the door open. A girl rose from behind a desk. She was a rather small girl with a nice figure, curly dark hair, very big and very blue eyes, and sweetly turned and very red lips. The head of the Westport Company evidently knew how to pick a charming secretary or receptionist, Slade decided.

'Vera,' said the sheriff, 'I want you to know a close friend of mine, Walt Slade. Walt, this is Miss Vera Allen, another friend of mine. She owns the Westport Company.'

SIX

To say Walt Slade was slightly flabbergasted would be putting it mildly. However, he dissembled his surprise and bowed with courtly grace over the hand the girl extended.

'I'm always very glad to meet one of the sheriff's friends,' she said in her soft, low voice.

'And I am sometimes amazed at the wonderful taste the sheriff shows when picking friends,' Slade replied, his eyes crinkling at the corners.

The girl laughed, showing white teeth and a dimple at the corner of her red mouth.

'That was nicely put,' she said. 'I fear, Mr. Slade, that you are addicted to flattery.'

'I am considered a very truthful person,' he answered.

Again the dimple. 'But is a man ever wholly truthful when conversing with a woman?' she asked.

'And that was ingenuously put,' he countered.

'Ingenuous can be defined either as free from dissimulation or artlessly frank,' was her answer. They laughed together.

'You two talk like a couple of dictionaries,' grumbled the sheriff. 'Trying to follow you is like trying to trail a tick through a sheep's wool.

'We just came from the inquest,' he added inconsequentially.

The girl's expression changed and there was pain in her blue eyes.

'Was anything more learned?' she asked. Davis shook his head.

'I feel terrible about it,' she said. 'I was just beginning to know Mr. Henderson well.'

'She's been here less than a month,' the sheriff interpolated.

'Yes,' the girl agreed. 'Mr. Henderson was not with the firm when it was located at Port Isabel. My uncle hired him after he moved its headquarters here, the first of last year. I recall him speaking highly of his ability. The whole thing is a horrible mystery. Why in the world was he out there in that boat?'

The sheriff shook his head. Slade studied the girl a moment.

'Do you know anything of Mr. Henderson's antecedents?' he asked.

Vera Allen shook her curly head. 'I don't recall him mentioning anything concerning his background,' she replied. 'He was evidently thoroughly familiar with the salvage and shipping business before he went to work for my uncle. I was satisfied with what I saw of his performance of his duties and never questioned him relative to his former experiences. Later, when I got to know him better, perhaps I would have. He was to an

49

extent an aloof individual and never appeared to hold much intercourse with the other employees.'

She hesitated, then said, 'I recall something my uncle once said of him, shortly before he died. He mentioned that Mr. Henderson was quite friendly with a certain ranch owner here of whom he did not approve. A Mr. Del Gregory, I believe it was.'

'Why didn't your uncle approve of Henderson's friendship with Gregory?' Slade asked. She smiled a trifle sadly.

'I fear my uncle was prejudiced against Gregory because he raises sheep,' she replied. 'Uncle Mitch was a former cattleman and had no use for sheep. Or for anybody who ran them onto the range, for that matter. I considered it silly, but he was old and, as the expression goes, set in his ways. He couldn't tolerate sheep and didn't want any part of them.'

'I see,' Slade said thoughtfully. He glanced at the litter of papers on her desk.

'We won't keep you from your work any longer,' he said. 'Thanks, very much, for receiving us.'

'It has been a pleasure,' she replied with emphasis. 'You'll come again?'

'I will,' Slade promised, also with emphasis. Sheriff Davis chuckled. And meeting the twinkle in his eyes, Vera Allen lowered her dark lashes, and the color in her creamily tanned cheeks deepened.

'Please do,' she said softly, to Slade.

Outside, the sheriff turned to his companion. 'Well, what do you think of her?' he asked.

'She's very charming,' Slade replied, 'but I've a notion she's shouldered a pretty hefty chore for a young girl—she can't be more than twenty-one or two.'

'Uh-huh, but she's a competent little body, and she's better fitted to handle the chore than you might think. She's thoroughly familiar with the business. She worked with her uncle, during summer vacations, for several years when the outfit was situated at Port Isabel, and I reckon old Mitch taught her plenty. She was away at school when he moved from Port Isabel and didn't show up here until shortly after his death, when it was learned she had inherited the business. Once she really gets the hang of things, I've a notion she's liable to make 'em hum. She's got good crews working the ships for her—old Mitch knew how to pick 'em. But I've a notion that in later years he didn't have the push Watson Payne of the Aransas has. Somehow, though, I got a feeling that Vera has, and will make Payne rattle his hocks to keep up with her before she's finished with him.'

'Could be,' Slade conceded. 'Never underestimate a woman.'

'I never have, that's why I've always fought

51

shy of 'em,' grunted the sheriff, a confirmed bachelor of past sixty.

'Why did Allen move his business from Port Isabel?' Slade asked.

'For the same reason Payne moved his here,' Davis replied. 'He 'lowed this was an up-and-coming town, that before all was said and done, and not too far off either, it would be not only a playground for tourists and such but one of the country's big ports with the trade fleets of all the world dropping anchor here. He said that on the black lands back of the town they'll be raising cotton by the million bales, and plenty of other garden truck that'll need shipping. And he said, with a lot of cuss words spikin' it, that sheep will be coming in, no keeping 'em out, and that Corpus Christi will be one of the country's big wool markets. So he figured he'd do well to get in on the ground floor.'

'He was right on all counts,' Slade said soberly. 'The years to come will show him to have been a prophet with honor in his own country.'

'Could be,' the sheriff conceded. 'Well, let's go get something to eat; all this palaver makes me hungry.'

At just about that time, Miss Vera Allen's elderly and cheerful office manager was asking a question somewhat similar to the one the sheriff had asked Slade, 'Well, what do you think of the notorious El Halcón?'

'I think,' Vera replied slowly, 'that he is the handsomest man I ever laid eyes on, and the most charming.'

'Careful,' warned the manager, 'there are folks say he's just an outlaw too smart to get caught.'

'I don't believe it,' Miss Allen said flatly. 'If he's an outlaw, how come Sheriff Davis is so friendly with him?'

'Oh, Slade always gets in with sheriffs,' the manager replied airily. 'That's because the sheriffs are always hoping to get something on him if they keep him hanging around close where they can keep an eye on him. Would be quite a feather in Davis' cap to drop a loop on El Halcón.'

Miss Allen's reaction could be characterized as nothing more dignified than a disdainful sniff.

'I think,' she said, 'that Berne Davis will have to get along without feathers, in his cap or elsewhere.

'But I think,' she added slowly, 'that he is more dangerous as he is than if he really was an outlaw.'

Just what she meant by that she did not explain, but the manager, with whom she had gotten on a very friendly basis during the month of her association with him, knew very well that the cryptic remark did *not* apply to Sheriff Berne Davis.

As they ate in a nearby restaurant, Slade regaled the sheriff with an account of the happening on the waterfront and the race between the rival tugs to reach the stranded steamer first. Davis listened with interest, glanced at his watch.

'There is liable to be a ruckus over there if those crews get together,' he remarked. 'It'll take a little time to float that tub. What say we ride over there and take a look? I figure I know where that reef is—this isn't the first time something has got hung up on it. Just about four or five miles from town.'

'Suits me,' Slade agreed. 'The operation should be interesting to watch, even if there is no trouble.'

Very quickly, they got the rigs on their horses and rode west by way of Comanche Street. It was a clear, bright day and the sand hills of Mustang Island across the gray-blue waters of the bay from Corpus Christi were clearly visible, lying on the horizon like tawny clouds.

The sun was well down the western slant of the sky when they reached the scene of operations, but there was still plenty of light. As they drew near, they saw that the steamer was resting slantwise on the reef and appeared to be firmly grounded. The only approach was by way of a narrow channel between two more reefs that showed under the clear water, so that only one tug at a time could operate. She had a line run to the steamer and was grunting and puffing and wallowing with no appreciable results. The steamer rocked and grated, and stayed right where it was.

'Hey!' Davis exclaimed, as they drew still nearer, 'that's one of the Westport tugs got the line on her. Looks like they got here first, after all. There's the Aransas down this way, lying close in shore.'

'And the other Westport tug is standing off and not able to lend a hand,' Slade commented.

A couple of dinghys were beached, one opposite the Aransas, the other across from where the steamer lay. By the first was a group of seamen who appeared to jeer at the Westport tug's futile efforts to dislodge the steamer. Standing by the Westport boat and bellowing orders was a burly individual with gray hair and a weatherbeaten face that at the moment looked very bad tempered.

'Hi, Hawkins,' the sheriff greeted him as they rode past the Aransas men, who regarded them in silence, and drew rein. 'So you got here first, eh?'

'Yep, we got here first,' the tug captain growled, casting a venomous glance at the Aransas men. 'The swab busted a steering line and had to heave to for repairs. They're sorta wrathy and might have tackled us if our other boat hadn't showed up and took the wind out of their canvas. We ain't doing much good so far, though. She's a tough one.'

Slade and the sheriff dismounted. Davis nodded to his companion. 'Walt,' he said, 'this is Skipper Si Hawkins of the Westport tug. Si, this is Walt Slade, an *amigo* of mine.'

'Sort of a heftier chore than ropin' a steer, eh, cowboy,' the skipper chuckled, jerking his head toward the laboring tug and the humming line as they shook hands.

'Well,' Slade smiled, 'if the steer were as clumsily roped as this operation is being conducted, it would quite likely be a hefty chore, too.'

The skipper bristled. 'What do you mean by that?' he demanded.

'I mean,' Slade replied, 'that you are not properly applying your power, and you'll never get her off the rocks the way you're going about it.'

'Is that so!' the skipper answered truculently. 'Maybe you could suggest a better way?'

'I can, if you wish me to,' Slade replied.

'Better listen to him, Si, he usually knows what he's talking about,' Sheriff Davis put in.

'All right! All right!' growled the skipper. 'I'm ready to listen to anything right now. But for a cowhand to tell me how to float a ship off a reef—well—'

'I don't mean to be presumptuous, Captain

56

Hawkins,' Slade said, 'but I do think I can offer a suggestion from which you might profit. Your warp is not properly applied, under the circumstances. You keep jerking up the stern of your tug and consequently losing power. Now here's what I would do—

'Out there in that channel is fairly deep water, and the bottom is mud, rather deep mud, unless I'm greatly mistaken. Drop your anchor—I see the hawse hole is pretty well back—then splice your warp to the anchor chain just above the waterline and go ahead at half-speed. The drag of the anchor will keep your stern down, increasing your power, and your power will be applied at the right angle to properly career your tow. I guarantee you'll have her off the reef in a jiffy.'

The old skipper stared at him. 'Son,' he said heavily, 'I'm darned if I don't believe it'll work. We'll sure give it a try.'

He began bellowing orders to the tug. There came an 'Aye, aye, sir!' The deckhands got busy. Very quickly all was in order. The skipper bellowed again, the tug puffed, the stack boomed. She lunged ahead. The warp hummed as it tightened.

The steamer lurched, swayed, grated and ground—and slid off the reef into deep water.

A resounding cheer went up from the decks of the two Westport tugs. It was echoed by a volley of angry exclamations and curses from the Aransas men. One detached himself from the group and strode forward with a rolling gait. He was a huge man with bristling red hair and angry eyes.

'That's Bledsoe, the Aransas skipper,' remarked Hawkins.

Bledsoe walked straight up to Slade. 'Blankety-blank you! Why'd you have to stick your bill in this?' he rumbled hoarsely.

Slade looked him up and down. 'Not much of a sportsman, are you, Captain?' he retorted in pleasantly conversational tones. 'Sort of a bad loser, eh?'

'I'll loser you!' yelled the skipper. His ponderous fist whizzed at Slade's face.

El Halcón moved his head slightly and the big fist slid harmlessly over his shoulder. Then a sizzling left hook laid the Aransas skipper's cheek open to the bone and sent him sprawling. He scrambled to his feet, gave a howl of rage and rushed forward, both fists flailing.

Slade hit him, left and right, to send him reeling back. He gathered himself together and rushed again. Slade glided forward to meet the rush, stepped on a pebble that rolled under his foot and staggered off balance. The skipper closed in on him, flinging his thick arms around his waist.

'He's got the under-holt!' whooped one of the Aransas men. 'That cowboy's a goner!'

SEVEN

He wasn't. Up came Slade's cupped hands, driving under the skipper's chin, forcing his head back and back despite his mighty efforts to swing his opponent off his feet, until the strain on the cervical spine was more than he could endure. He loosened his hold, staggered free. And Slade hit him with all his two hundred pounds of muscular weight behind the blow. The skipper went down, and this time he stayed down.

The Aransas men howled their anger. Slade's hands moved like the flicker of a hawk's wing. The crash of a shot quivered the air. A man who had furtively drawn a gun gave a scream of pain and doubled up, gripping his blood-spurting hand between his knees. The gun lay half a dozen yards away. The Aransas men stared into two black muzzles, one wisping smoke. And back of those rock-steady muzzles were the terrible eyes of El Halcón.

'Anyone else in the notion of fanging?' Slade asked pleasantly. 'I aim to accommodate.' The group cringed away from him.

It had all happened so quickly that Sheriff Davis hadn't had time to swing into action. Now he let out a stentorian roar and strode forward, shaking his fist at the Aransas men.

'One more yip out of any of you and I'll throw the lot of you in the calaboose and keep you there till you trip over your whiskers!' he boomed. 'Into your boat and get going.' He whirled on the Aransas skipper, who was sitting up, looking dazed and rubbing his bloody face.

'On your feet, Bledsoe, and trail your twine with the rest of your hooligans,' he said. 'Git, I said!'

Bledsoe staggered to his feet, shot Slade a vicious look. 'I'll be seeing *you*,' he threatened.

'Look close the first time, you might not get a chance for a second,' Slade advised.

Muttering and mumbling, the skipper piled into the dinghy, to which the wounded man, groaning and cursing, had been escorted by two of his companions. The oars flashed and the little boat pulled away from the shore. Slade sauntered to the water's edge to closely watch the departure, although he did not really think any further inimical move would be made.

Captain Hawkins turned to the sheriff. 'Say, he's some feller!' he exclaimed. 'He ain't no cowhand, is he?'

'Well, not exactly, although he's worked at being one, at times,' Davis replied.

'Ain't a seaman, either, though I've a notion he knows plenty about it,' Hawkins added. 'But I'll tell you I bet I know what he is—an engineer, and a darned good one. Only an engineer could figure out those warp and water and bottom conditions like he did. He is an engineer, ain't he, Berne?'

'Yes, I guess he is,' the sheriff admitted.

*   *   *

The sheriff and the captain were right. Shortly before the death of his father, which occurred after financial reverses that entailed the loss of the elder Slade's ranch, young Walt had graduated from a famous college of engineering. He had planned to take a post-graduate course to round out his education and better fit him for the profession he had determined to make his life's work. That for the moment being out of the question, he had lent an attentive ear when Captain Jim McNelty, his father's friend, with whom he had worked during summer vacations, suggested that he come into the Rangers for a while and pursue his studies in spare time.

Long since he had gotten more through private study than he could have hoped for from the post-grad. In the meantime, however, Ranger work had gotten a strong hold on him and he was reluctant to sever connections with the illustrious corps of peace officers. He was still young, plenty of time to be an engineer; he'd stick with the Rangers for a while.

*   *   *

'Well, reckon we might as well be moving, too,' Hawkins said as they watched the Aransas tug storm off for Corpus Christi. He turned to Slade, who had returned, holding the damaged gun he shot out of the Aransas man's hand.

'Much obliged, son, for what you did,' he said. 'I won't forget it, and I've a notion the Company will want to express gratitude in a more substantial way. I'll relay the word of what happened to the office.'

'Thank you, Captain Hawkins,' Slade replied seriously, but with laughter in his eyes. Sheriff Davis, who understood, repressed a chuckle.

Hawkins was rowed to his boat and a few minutes later the tug got under way with her tow; sailors aboard the damaged steamer waving goodbye to Slade and the sheriff.

'Note the calibre of the iron that sidewinder pulled,' Slade remarked to Davis.

The sheriff took the arm, one butt plate of which was shattered, and examined it.

'Forty-one,' he remarked. 'Sort of unusual for this section.'

'Very unusual,' Slade agreed. 'May mean nothing, but keep it in mind.'

Davis nodded, and, glanced at the sunset sky. 'Hadn't we better be heading for town?'

he suggested.

'Just a minute,' Slade replied. He walked again to the water's edge, this time to the verge of the channel of deep water, studying it, his black brows drawing together until the concentration furrow was deep between them, a sure sign that El Halcón was doing some hard thinking.

'Strange that the steamer should have slammed slantwise across that reef like she did,' he remarked in a musing voice. 'This channel runs right to the shore and is plenty deep. Deep enough for her to nose in close enough to perhaps unload some cargo. Shouldn't have had any trouble doing it, especially with a skipper or pilot who knows the coast. I've a notion she was heading into the channel when she struck. Well, it's high tide now, but I think I'll have another look tomorrow when the tide is at ebb. Interesting.'

Sheriff Davis shot him a puzzled glance, but refrained from asking questions that he doubtless felt would not be answered. In which he was right.

'Let's go,' Slade said. 'Now I'm really hungry.'

'Me, too,' the sheriff agreed heartily as he forked his horse.

It was a very pleasant evening and they took their time on the way back to town, discussing the recent happenings.

'First time I ever knew that Aransas bunch

to start anything like real trouble,' the sheriff remarked. 'Oh, some of them have had a mite of a ruckus with the Westport hands now and then, but nothing worth bothering with. Bledsoe, the skipper of that tug, is a rough character but usually behaves himself fairly well. Guess he got a larrupin' today he'll remember for a while. You sure handled him neat, and he's got a reputation for being an ugly customer at rough and tumble.'

'Might do very well at it if he'd learn to tighten the *látigo* on his temper,' Slade replied. 'As it was, he laid himself wide open every move he made.'

'And you sure laid his face wide open for him,' chuckled Davis. 'He was bleeding like a stuck pig. Keep an eye out for him, though. Wouldn't put it past him to take advantage of you if he got a chance.'

Slade nodded but did not otherwise comment. His thoughts were busy with something other than Captain Bledsoe's possible hankering for revenge.

When they reached Corpus Christi after a leisurely ride, they saw that the Westport tug and her tow were already docked.

'The boys will have quite a yarn to spin in the Matagorda tonight,' Davis chuckled. 'Let's go eat.'

A restaurant on Lipan Street provided a tasty meal of which both partook with eagerness.

'And now,' said Davis, 'I'll amble over and let Cliff, the deputy, go eat. Coming along?'

'Might as well,' Slade agreed.

When they entered the office, the deputy said, 'Mack Russell of the Westport Company was here a little while ago looking for Slade. Left a note for him.' He passed an unsealed envelope to the Ranger.

Drawing forth the single sheet it contained, Slade read,

Dear Mr. Slade:
Would you please drop in at the office, if convenient. I'll be there until ten.
Sincerely,
(signed)   Vera Allen

'Now what?' Slade wondered, passing the note to Davis, who perused it with frowning brows.

'Hard to tell what a woman wants,' was his comment. 'Better watch your step; you'd be safer ambling into a catamount's hole-up.' He glanced at the clock. 'Twenty minutes till ten right now; you've got time to make it, if you aim to take a chance.'

'Guess I will,' Slade replied, pocketing the note and heading for the door.

When he reached the Westport building, he found Vera Allen seated in the outer office, shapely legs comfortably crossed.

'Hello?' she greeted. 'Was just about ready

to give you up; was afraid my note had miscarried. I hope you won't consider me presumptuous but I really do wish to talk to you. Sit down, won't you?'

Slade drew the chair a bit closer and sat down. 'Not at all,' he replied to her remark. 'It beautifully brightened a dull day.'

'Dull?' she repeated. 'I fear your notions of what is dull and mine don't agree. Captain Hawkins was here just before I wrote that note, and from what he told me I'd say you had a rather lively day. His account of what you did for us was glowing, to put it mildly.'

'I fear the good captain stopped at the Matagorda, and as a result his description acquired a somewhat alcoholic flavor,' Slade replied. Vera shook her head.

'He didn't appear affected by what he may have imbibed,' she differed. 'And there is a saying, you know, "Out of wine cometh truth". I've a notion today is a good example. Really, though, he greatly appreciated what you did, and so do I.'

'It was a privilege and a pleasure to have the opportunity to lend a hand,' he answered.

Vera smiled. 'You have a wonderful gift for saying just the right thing,' she said. 'Incidentally, what's the Matagorda you mentioned?'

'A saloon and restaurant where the seamen drink, down on Water Street,' he replied. Vera looked interested.

'Speaking of seamen, that brings me to what I wish to talk to you about,' she said. 'Captain Hawkins voiced the opinion that you have had considerable experience with the sea and seamen.'

'I would hardly say considerable, but some,' he conceded.

'I think you are given to deprecating your accomplishments,' she said. 'As you know, I own the Westport Company. I'm thoroughly conversant with all the angles of the business, but after all I am a woman.'

'A conclusion at which I arrived some time ago,' he smiled. 'My vision is still fairly unclouded.'

Under his laughing regard she dimpled, and blushed a little, gave a furtive tug to the hem of her skirt and desisted, blushing a little more, as his laughter spilled over.

'As you are aware,' she resumed, 'cowhands have an absurd aversion to working for a woman boss. The same applies to seamen, even more so. Because of which I don't think I'm getting the very best from my crews; they need a man over them to keep them on their toes. Mr. Slade, would you consider taking over the management of the Westport Company, at least for a while?'

EIGHT

Slade hesitated a moment, visioning certain complications that were very likely to develop. However, the offer did not lack attractions. It would give him an excellent excuse for remaining in the section and would keep him in constant touch with the waterfront, which he was positive was the focus of the trouble he had been sent to investigate.

'Subject to a condition,' he tentatively accepted.

'A condition?'

'Yes. That I am free to handle the chore as I think best, without interference from anybody, including the owner.'

It was Vera's turn to hesitate. 'I think,' she said slowly, 'that you would not tolerate interference by a woman under any circumstances.'

'If you were six feet tall instead of about five, weighed two hundred pounds instead of around a hundred, and wore a handlebar mustache, the condition would still remain, so far as business relations are concerned, which are conducted on a strictly impersonal basis. Otherwise, the lady confers.'

She laughed outright at that. 'I also think,' she said, 'that you would not be satisfied with conferment.'

'Very well, let's make it *concurs*,' he replied, looking her squarely in the eyes.

This time she really did blush, and hurriedly changed the subject.

'And your salary?'

Slade shrugged. 'You're doing the hiring.'

She named a figure. He nodded and did not otherwise comment. Miss Allen put that ready acquiescence into the back of her mind for future reference.

'So that takes care of that,' she said. 'You'll take charge immediately?'

There was laughter in his eyes when he replied. 'Tomorrow. Tonight you're not yet my boss. Have you been here all day?'

'Yes,' she admitted. 'I stayed on late hoping to contact you.

'You must be tired. And aren't you hungry? You haven't had your dinner?'

'No,' she answered, 'and I'm famished.'

'We'll take care of that,' he promised. 'I've already eaten, but I'll have coffee and maybe a slab of pie with you. By the way, don't you think you're taking something of a chance, bestowing such responsibility on one who is almost a stranger to you?' he added as they stood up.

'I'm not worried,' she replied blithely. 'I think I can judge people fairly well, and the recommendations of Captain Hawkins and Sheriff Davis certainly left nothing to be desired. 'Gracious! how tall you are! I'd have to stand on tiptoe to—to—' She stopped, blushing hotly.

'Don't let that bother you, it can easily be remedied,' he reassured her. 'And you're not my boss tonight.'

'And I doubt if I ever will be,' she said. 'I'm afraid you don't take to bossing very well.'

'Depends on who is doing the bossing and what the circumstances,' he replied. 'Any place in particular where you'd like to eat?'

'I've a notion the Matagorda you spoke of wouldn't be bad,' she answered.

Slade hesitated.

'Sort of rough down there at times,' he demurred.

Miss Allen shrugged daintily. 'Oh, I've been to rough places before, with my uncle,' she said. 'I don't mind, and it sounds interesting.'

'Okay,' he agreed. 'But don't complain if something happens to make your hair even curlier than it is now.'

'Don't you like curly hair?' she asked.

'Using a flamboyant expression, I adore it.'

'Then here's to curlier curls,' she answered. 'Let's go!'

Slade tucked her arm in his and they set out. It was a pleasant walk to the Matagorda and they sauntered along leisurely, Vera apparently forgetting her hunger for the moment, for she set the pace.

There were stares when they entered the saloon. Bert Hobart, the fiercely mustached owner hurried forward, bowing and smiling, and escorted them to a table near the dance-floor.

'It's a pleasure, Miss Allen, a great pleasure to have you with us,' he said. 'And Mr. Slade, ain't it? Captain Hawkins has been sounding off about you all evening. There he is at the bar, looking this way. Waiter, everything the best.'

'Thank you, very much,' Vera replied. 'It's a pleasure to be with you.' She beckoned the skipper, who came rolling across the room looking a bit bewildered.

'Join us for a few minutes, Captain,' Vera said, motioning to a chair. 'I have something to tell you.'

The captain sat down, diffidently, and looked expectant.

'Captain, you are to a large extent responsible for what's happened,' Vera said. The captain looked startled, and somewhat apprehensive.

'Now what have I done?' he asked.

'Nothing but what you should be proud of,' Vera told him. 'You've just acquired a new Admiral of the fleet.'

'Wh-what!' exclaimed the astounded mariner.

'Yes,' Vera said, 'I've hired Mr. Slade to take over the management of the Westport Company. What do you think?'

The skipper gurgled with astonishment,

then he said, 'I think, Ma'am, that some swabs I know of will think that a Gulf hurricane has just come up abaft them, with shoaling waters ahead.'

Vera laughed merrily. 'What a reputation you have, Mr. Slade,' she said. 'You must be a terrible person, although you seem so nice and gentle.'

'Didn't I tell you the captain is prone to exaggeration,' Slade protested. Vera smiled.

'I believe we have two of the three tugs and two steamers in port, have we not?' Vera observed. 'Mr. Slade will visit them tomorrow, Captain. Tell your boys to have everything shipshape.'

'They'd better,' the captain predicted ominously.

'Have a drink with us and then spread the word around,' Vera added.

'I'll do that, Ma'am,' the captain promised. He downed his drink when it arrived and hurried to the bar.

Although undoubtedly greatly surprised at the Westport owner's visit to the place, the cowhands and seamen at the bar and elsewhere in the room, after their initial astonishment, quickly turned back to their various activities and paid the couple at the table no mind.

'Cowhands and seamen have something in common,' Slade remarked. 'Great respect for a nice woman.'

'Nice or not nice are relative, are they not?' Vera observed.

'Largely a matter of personal viewpoint,' Slade replied.

'Or impersonal?'

'Exactly.'

They laughed together.

*　　*　　*

Captain Hawkins was circulating like hot water. Once again glances were shot at the table.

'But they're looking at you, not me,' Vera giggled, her eyes dancing.

'Oh, they manage to ricochet a glance in your direction at the same time,' Slade replied. 'Who can blame them!'

'With all those pretty girls on the dance-floor!' she scoffed.

'All those *other* pretty girls would phrase it better,' he answered.

'Thank you, sir,' she said demurely. 'Thank goodness my dinner is here! Another moment and I'd have toppled over. You just having coffee and pie?'

'I told you I'd just put away a hefty surrounding,' he replied.

'A man of your inches should always be hungry,' she declared, as she addressed herself to her own food.

'And now I feel a lot better,' she said, a little

later. 'Those dance-floor girls *are* pretty,' she added, smiling and waving to one that passed close by.

'As I said, this place can be rather rough at times, but I understand it has a reputation for good food and drinks, straight games, and girls who are square-shooters,' Slade commented. 'From the look of the owner, I've a notion he wouldn't put up with any other kind. It pays off in the end.'

'The food was wonderful and I think the girls are nice,' Vera replied. 'I wouldn't know about the games or the drinks.'

'I can hardly introduce you to the games at the moment, but how, about a drink?' he suggested.

'Just one,' she accepted. 'I have to watch my complexion.'

'I would say you have watched it very closely,' he complimented, and was rewarded with a smile and a dimple.

They had the drink. Then Vera asked, 'Would it be permissable for us to dance?'

'Of course,' he answered. 'That's what the floor's for.'

'Then let's,' she said, jumping to her feet. He led her to the floor and encircled her trim waist with a long arm.

Walt Slade liked to dance and he could dance, and in Miss Vera Allen he had found a fit partner. Soon the other dancers drew aside to watch their performance, and when the number was finished there was a spontaneous burst of applause, to which they bowed acknowledgment.

'You were wonderful,' she said breathlessly, for the number had been a fast one. 'Is there anything you don't do well?'

'We'll leave that in abeyance for you to pass judgment,' he answered. Vera lowered her lashes.

When they reached the table, she said, 'Don't you think we'd better be going? It's late and we've both had a long day.'

'It ended a very pleasant one for me,' he replied.

'Me, too,' she said. 'I don't know when I've enjoyed an evening so much.'

They waved goodbye and left the saloon, a chorus of well missible for us to dance?

As they approached the nearby alley mouth, Slade suddenly thrust his companion behind him.

'Stay back there,' he snapped. 'Obey me!'

The bewildered girl did as she was told. Slade took a long stride forward; he was ready when the four men darted from the alley mouth and threw themselves upon him. He had drawn both guns, but he didn't pull trigger. Instead, he slashed left and right with the heavy barrels. The cold steel and the knife-edged sights crunched and ripped on bone and flesh. Screams of pain arose. The attack was thrown into confusion. And before the drygulchers could catch their balance, out of the saloon streamed the Westport seamen and their cowhand companions, whooping encouragement.

The attackers incontinently took to their heels up the alley, the crowd bellowing after them, but soon outdistanced.

'You all right?' Captain Hawkins, who had remained behind, asked Vera anxiously.

'I'm fine,' she replied. 'You all right, Walt?'

'Fine as frog hair,' was Slade's cheerful rejoinder as he holstered his guns. Hawkins mopped his perspiring face.

'I wouldn't have had this happen for a million,' he declared. 'I hope you weren't too bad scared, Miss Allen.'

'I didn't have time to be scared,' Vera replied. 'Really, I think I rather enjoyed it.'

Hawkins gazed at her admiringly. 'Ma'am, excuse me for saying it, but you're the kind of a lass I'd want to have next me on the quarter with a China Sea typhoon bearin' down.'

'Thank you, Captain,' Vera replied simply, and sincerely. Hawkins turned his admiration to Slade.

'And son, you're a wonder!' he said. 'The way you keel-hauled those swabs! Betcha it was Bledsoe and some of his galley sweepings.'

'Possibly,' Slade conceded. 'I didn't get a good look at any faces. They had caps pulled down low and handkerchiefs muffed up.

But I think I left a few distinguishing marks on them.'

'You sure did!' chortled Hawkins. 'They took quite a few between wind and water. Why didn't you shoot?'

'Because I didn't think they were out to do a killing,' Slade replied. 'Would have been taking an unfair advantage, as it were.'

Hawkins shook his grizzled head dubiously but didn't argue.

The seamen and the cowhands came drifting back down the alley, talking excitedly. They grinned and bobbed and filed back into the saloon.

'Thanks, boys,' Slade called after them. 'You were a help.'

'You didn't need no help, we were just trying to help those swabs get away while they could still navigate. We felt sorry for them,' a voice called, amid a gale of laughter.

'Well, guess the excitement is over,' Slade said. 'Good-night, Captain, see you tomorrow.'

As they left the waterfront Slade said, 'Well, after tonight, I've a very strong notion your boys are going to be bragging about their Lady Boss and ready to wallop anybody who makes a disparaging remark about her being a woman.'

'I hope so,' Vera sighed. 'I'll admit I was getting a little discouraged. And if it is so, I have you to thank for it.'

'I just provided you an opportunity to show the boys what you really are,' he replied. 'That's all you needed to do. Now they're for you from jib to keelson.'

Vera glanced at him with laughing eyes. 'You are quite familiar with nautical terms, I see,' she said. 'But applied to a woman, the implication can be slightly—startling.'

With laughter in his own eyes, he glanced down at the trim little figure beside him and answered, 'In this particular instance, startlingly true,' which 'implication' caused Miss Allen to forego repartee, for the moment at least, dealing with that particular subject.

The walk up town was uneventful. Vera paused before a trim little house set in a yard on Gavilan Street.

'Here's where I live,' she said. 'It was Uncle Mitch's place. Small but comfortable.'

He saw her to the door and opened it for her. She paused again before entering, looking up at him.

'And now to bed with you,' he said. 'You've had quite a day. Do as I tell you; I'm still Boss for a few hours.'

'And always will be, I hope,' she said softly.

He cupped his hands around her slender waist, lifted her from the ground until her face was on a level with his. She wound her arms about his neck and her lips clung to his in a goodnight kiss.

'Strictly impersonal,' she giggled as he

dropped her back on her feet. 'Good—night!'
She closed the door, very softly.

*　　　*　　　*

Before retiring, Slade stopped to commune
with Shadow for a moment.

'Well, horse, I don't know what I'm letting
myself in for, but it is interesting,' he said.

Shadow blew resignedly through his nose,
as much as to say, 'Here we go again!'

Slade chuckled, and went to bed.

NINE

When Vera arrived at the office, she found
Mack Russell already at work.

'Well, what do you think of my acquisition?'
she asked. Russell shrugged.

'Excellent, so far as the business is
concerned,' he conceded.

'And what do you mean by that, "so far as
the business is concerned?"'

The elderly office man gave her a paternal
look. 'Reckon you know enough Spanish to
translate what the Mexicans call him?'

'El Halcón—The Hawk,' she answered.

'Well,' Russell returned dryly, 'it isn't easy
to cage and tame a hawk.'

'Who said anything about caging and

79

taming him?'

Russell smiled but did not otherwise comment. 'Guess I'd better amble around and see how the boys in the other offices are making out,' he said. 'A lot of work to do today. Incidentally, the company who owns that steamer is making a nice salvage payment, thanks to your hawk.'

Vera followed his departing back with her eyes. 'Dam him, he hardly ever makes a mistake,' she told the typewriter on the desk.

The typewriter, unresponsive, did not deign to so much as click a key. Vera made a face at it and fixed her gaze on the window that overlooked the street. Her eyes were still regarding the street expectantly when Russell returned to his office.

'There's one thing puzzled me a bit,' she remarked. 'He didn't seem the least interested in what his pay would be. If I'd said five dollars a week, I've a notion he would have taken the job just as readily.'

Russell regarded her with laughing eyes. 'Well?' he observed pointedly.

Vera blushed hotly and bit her lip. Then her sense of humor came to the rescue and she laughed with him.

'I fear you overestimate me, Uncle Mack,' she said. Russell chuckled.

'Nope, I don't think I do,' he replied. 'And I'm willing to bet he doesn't *under*estimate you.'

Which ended a conversation that had lasted long enough.

*   *   *

When Slade arrived, a little later, she was waiting for him.

'Come here,' she ordered. 'I'm the Boss, now.' She led him to the inner office and closed the door.

'Now bend your tall head,' she directed, and stood on tip toe. 'There! that pays back the one you gave me last night.'

'I demand interest on the debt,' he insisted, and got it.

'And now, if it's all right with you, I'm going down to the waterfront and look things over,' he said.

'Anything you wish to do, dear, is all right with me,' she conceded.

'Anything?'

She blushed, but met his eyes.

'Anything!'

Arriving at the waterfront, Slade found Captain Hawkins standing at the foot of the gangplank that led to the deck of his tug. Expectant faces leaned over the rail. The same obtained on the second tug and a couple of small steamers moored nearby.

'All set for inspection,' chuckled the captain. 'The boys are all ears.'

First, Slade inspected the captain's tug.

81

Decks were snowy-white, woodwork and plates painted, not a sign of rust.

'Excellent,' he complimented the skipper. 'Couldn't be better. An old deep-water man, aren't you, Captain?'

'That's right,' Hawkins replied. 'Put in at most ports over the world. Around old Cape Stiff seven times.'

'Once around Cape Horn is a chore,' Slade said. 'Well, here goes for the next tub.'

The second tug also proved to be in satisfactory condition, as was the first steamer he investigated. It was different with the second steamer, the Albatross. She was dirty, and there was an odor which, mixed as it was with the smell of bilge and tar and stale cooking, was hard to define, but which Slade found distinctly unpleasant. He took one look and turned to the skipper who had the appearance of being a good man but a bit too easy-going.

'Call your crew together,' he ordered. When the deckhands had assembled, some of whom, he noted, had been in the Matagorda the night before, he addressed them sternly and to the point, 'This ship is a mess. She's a disgrace to the Westport Company. I want these decks holystoned till they're white. I want the woodwork and the plates repainted, at once, and when I come back here late in the afternoon, I don't want to see any signs of rust. Do you understand?'

The crew, taking a good look at him and recalling his performance of the night before, evidently 'understood.' Even before he descended the gangplank, all hands were busily at work.

'You've got 'em,' Hawkins, who had accompanied him on his tour of inspection, chuckled. 'They're all right, and so is Vane, the skipper, but he's sort of an easy-going swab and inclined to be a bit lax, and so is his mate. So it ain't strange that the boys get a mite careless. I figure things will be different from now on.'

'They'd better be,' Slade said grimly. 'Let's see, now, I understand there are two more steamers out to sea, and another tug.'

'That's right,' nodded Hawkins. 'Tug's on its way from Brownsville right now,'

'I'll look them over when they make port,' Slade said. 'And now, what's the line-up for your tugs today?'

'In a couple of hours or so we expect to warp the Compostella into her slip; she's a big one. Then this afternoon we'll ease the Yorkshire away from the wharf; she's another big one. Figure Westport Three will get here from Brownsville in time to lend a hand. That's the Yorkshire right down the line.'

Slade nodded and gazed at the towering steamer. 'And when you have a tug free, send it cruising to the west,' he directed. 'Might run onto something profitable over there.'

'Yes?' The skipper looked puzzled.

'Yes,' Slade answered, without explaining. He was thinking of the peculiar mishap to the steamer that straddled the reef the day before. He had resolved to ride west the next day and have a look at the channel, where she had come to grief.

'Wonder where Bledsoe's Aransas tug is?' he remarked.

'Don't know,' replied Hawkins. 'She and the other Aransas tug steamed out past Mustang Island early this morning, evidently bound for the Gulf. I tried to get a look at her deckhands but they seemed to sorta keep out of sight. I think I did see one with a rag tied around his head. He had something to remember you by, I've a notion.'

'Could be,' Slade conceded.

'Hey!' exclaimed Hawkins. 'Here comes Watson Payne who owns the Aransas Company. Wonder what he wants? Big feller, ain't he?'

Payne waved a greeting and approached. 'I'm sorry, Mr. Slade, for what happened yesterday out there by the reef,' he said when he was within speaking distance. 'I gave Bledsoe a good dressing down. He's all right, but he's hot tempered and apt to fly off the handle too easily. His men are loyal to him, which accounts for the second action you were forced to take. I hope there are no hard feelings over what happened.'

'None at all so far as I'm concerned, over what happened out by the reef,' Slade replied.

'Glad to hear it,' said Payne. 'I'll guarantee it won't happen again.' With a smile and a nod he walked on.

Hawkins shot Slade a shrewd glance. 'Notice you didn't mention what happened last night, which I've a notion you don't feel quite so forgiving about,' he observed.

'We have no proof that any of the Aransas men had a hand in that,' Slade reminded him. Hawkins gave a derisive snort, for which Slade did not reprove him.

An hour before noon, the Compostella nosed around the point of Mustang Island and the cheerful, puffing tugs skillfully warped her into place. Slade was impressed by the competent handling of the two little vessels and complimented the skippers and the crews.

Meanwhile Westport Three put in an appearance, helped ease the Yorkshire out and sent her on her way to blue water.

Later, Slade paid his promised return visit to the untidy steamer. There he found everything shipshape and showing the effects of plenty of hard work. The unpleasant and hard to define odor still lingered but was much less pronounced. Doubtless due to some cargo she had carried, he decided.

Turning to the skipper, Slade said, 'Captain, break out a bottle or two and serve a double tot of grog to all hands.'

Somebody shouted, 'Hurrah for the Admiral!' The cheer was given heartily amid a gale of laughter. Slade flashed his white smile and waved acknowledgment.

'What an admiral *he* would make,' Captain Hawkins observed to his mate, another oldster retired from deep water and an educated man.

'Yes,' agreed the mate. 'He has that something which would inspire other men to follow him to the death.'

'And they'd have to follow darn fast to keep up with him,' grunted Hawkins.

It was late when Slade returned to the office, but he found Vera there, waiting for him.

'And I'm starved,' she declared plaintively. 'You'll be the death of me, the hours you keep. Everybody else has gone home, long ago.'

'The Boss's work is never done,' he replied. 'Where'd you like to eat, the Matagorda?'

'Of course,' she replied. 'My boys will be there, won't they?'

'I expect quite a few of them will be,' he admitted. 'All except those who are tied up with something. Let's go.'

The Matagorda was crowded. When they entered, grins and nods and a waving of hands greeted them.

'You're accepted,' Slade chuckled as the proprietor, with a twirl of his mustache, escorted them to a table. 'Just one of the boys.'

'Huh!' Vera sniffed. 'I'm no such thing.'

'Metaphorically speaking, not literally,' he smiled.

They had a very pleasant dinner together, for both were hungry with the hunger of youth and perfect health, and did full justice to the repast. As they lingered over final cups of coffee, Slade noticed an old cowhand make his way to the orchestra leader and say a few words that caused the leader to smile and nod. He had a very good notion what was coming.

'Prepare to take some punishment,' he told his companion. 'I'll hardly be able to refuse.'

'What do you mean?' she asked, her big eyes widening.

'You'll see,' he answered as the leader borrowed a guitar from one of his musicians and headed for the table. He arrived with a smile and a deep bow and held out the instrument suggestively.

'Will not the *Cápitan* sing for us?' he asked in a persuasive voice. 'As he did for me once in Laredo? I have never forgotten.'

'I thought your face looked familiar,' Slade replied.

'Can he really sing?' Vera asked, her eyes widening again.

'*Sangre de Cristo! Señorita*, can he sing!' exclaimed the leader. 'If you have tears to shed, prepare to shed them. Even the rattlesnake and the horned toad do so when

El Halcón sings!'

'I don't know whether I should take that as a compliment or not,' Vera said with a giggle as Slade stood up and accepted the guitar.

With the leader proudly clearing the way, Slade walked to the little raised platform that accommodated the orchestra and turned to face the suddenly expectant crowd. The leader's voice rang out, '*Señoritas* and *Señores!* the great honor is done us. *El Cápitan* will sing!'

Slade ran his fingers over the strings with crisp power, played a soft prelude, then threw back his black head and sang—first a chantey of the sea,

Night! and a wild wind blowing!
Thunder of tide on the bar!
And God's great poem, the firmament,
Unrolling star by star . . .

And as the great golden metallic baritone-bass pealed and rang through the room, all activities ceased and all eyes were fixed on the singer. When the music ceased with a crash of chords, tumultuous applause followed, and shouts for another.

Slade caught the old cowhand's eye, smiled and nodded, and sang a rollicking ballad of the range. He finished the performance with a hauntingly sweet love song of old *Méjico*, bowed to the applause and returned to his table.

'That orchestra leader was right,' Vera said, wiping her eyes with a wispy handkerchief. 'Another accomplishment! Is there anything you can't do, and do well?'

'And we'll leave that in abeyance, too,' he replied.

Soon afterward they left the saloon, for it was late and both had had a long day. The walk back uptown under the stars was peaceful, and when they reached the house on Gavilan Street, *they* closed the door, softly.

TEN

When Vera arrived for work the next day, old Mack Russell, the office manager, shot her a shrewd glance.

'Hmmm!' he said. 'See the roses are blooming in your cheeks this morning. Still think you can cage him?'

'I think I have a better chance than I did have,' she retorted and hurried to her inner sanctum as the 'roses' bloomed brighter, leaving old Mack chuckling.

Slade visited the waterfront but briefly to confer a few minutes with Captain Hawkins. He repaired to the livery stable, got the rig on Shadow and rode west, following the route he and Sheriff Davis had taken a couple of days before. When he reached the channel where the steamer got into trouble, he dismounted and approached the water, which was low, very clear, and almost motionless, the tide being at close to ebb.

He noted several ships well out on the bay, and one that looked like a tug speeding west. He paid them little mind for none turned in his direction.

One of the reefs was exposed for some distance. He walked out onto it and stood for some time studying the water of the channel before he returned to his horse.

'Just as I figured, Shadow,' he said. 'The channel's blocked. Somebody tumbled a lot of big boulders into it, must have been quite a chore. The steamer, thinking she had plenty of draught, barged into the channel as she was accustomed to doing, hit the obstruction, spun around and straddled the reef. That's why her bow was somewhat stove up, not from the reef, as everybody supposed.'

He paused to roll and light a cigarette and resumed, 'Lucky it happened that way, I expect. Otherwise it might have knocked a hole in her and sunk her, with a possible loss of life. Well, looks like we've got our work cut out for us, if this is a sample how the hellions work. A snake-blooded outfit for fair. So far we haven't anything but suspicion, but maybe we'll get a break. Certain angles aren't working out too bad. Among other things, I'm all set for water transportation if I happen to need it. You haven't enough duck in you to be much good out on the bay. Well, you can put your particular talents to use right now.'

Pinching out the butt, he tossed it aside, mounted and headed back to town, heavy with thought.

One unanswered question at the moment irritated him more than the others. What was the mysterious deal between the sheep raiser, Del Gregory, and the murdered purchasing agent, Malcolm Henderson? That Vera Allen knew nothing about it he was positive; so just what was Henderson doing unbeknownst to the owner of the company for which he worked? Slade had a notion that whatever it was, its inception quite likely was before she took over the outfit. Perhaps old Mitch Allen, her uncle and the former owner, had been aware of what Henderson had in mind and had condoned it. Possibly the purchasing agent feared the new head of the company, a woman, would not approve of the transaction but had felt obligated to go through with it. Perhaps at the insistence of Gregory, with whom it seemed he had been on friendly terms. So Henderson acted without her knowledge, quite likely convinced that it was to the advantage of the company to do so. Then he possibly had intended to juggle his accounts so that the emolument to the company would appear to have come from some other source.

For the time being at least, Slade did not think that Henderson had been out to line his own pockets, with Gregory a fellow conspirator. No matter what else Del Gregory might be, he did not strike the Ranger as being the sort that would go in for larceny in any of its forms. And what he had learned of Henderson inclined him to believe that the late purchasing agent had been an honest man.

All supposition, of course, but at the moment that was all he had to go on. Perhaps developments would tend to substantiate his deductions.

At any rate, he was formulating a nebulous theory, flimsily foundationed, so far, as to what was going on in the section. Which was something. Well, a talk with Vera Allen and another one with Captain Si Hawkins might help.

Another unanswered question was more ominous, especially where he was personally concerned: Who killed Malcolm Henderson? He knew that until that question was answered and the culprits brought to justice, he was in continuous danger. There was no doubt but that the drygulching of Del Gregory was a case of mistaken identity; the drygulchers were after El Halcón, not Gregory, who very nearly got his comeuppance in consequence. The men who brought Henderson's body to shore had gotten a good enough look at him, Slade, to be able to recognize him when they next saw him. It was logical that they wouldn't want a witness to their landing. Also, very probably he had later been recognized by them as El Halcón with a reputation for horning in on good things others had going. Which would tend to step up their campaign against him. And their advantage lay in the fact that they knew whom they were gunning for while he had no definite notion as to whom to keep an eye on. Oh, well, things usually worked out and doubtless would again.

A sudden explosive snort from Shadow brought him back to his immediate surroundings. Ahead the trail ran straight for nearly a mile. To the right was the bay, but a short distance away. On his left was a long slope running up from the trail. For about a thousand yards it was covered by a heavy stand of chaparral, after which the growth thinned rapidly before reaching the crest, which was bare. He twisted in his saddle to look back. Some six or seven hundred yards to the rear a band of four horsemen were riding toward him at a fast clip. He studied them a moment. Could be only a bunch of cowhands heading for town. He spoke to Shadow and the big horse quickened his gait. The bunch behind also speeded up. A puff of whitish smoke mushroomed from their ranks. A bullet sang past overhead.

'So, want to play, eh?' Slade remarked as he turned back to the front. 'Well, we'll see about that. Trail Shadow, trail!'

Instantly the black horse extended himself, his hoofs drumming the trail. He tossed his head, slugged it above the bit, snorted, and fairly poured his long body over the ground.

More bullets whined by, none coming close. Six hundred yards was long shooting distance, especially from the back of a galloping horse.

'Just the same there's something funny about this,' Slade told the cayuse. He twisted in the saddle and gazed back; the pursuit was already losing ground. But they kept on shooting.

And then abruptly there wasn't a darn thing funny about it. A slug whined past, close, and it came from the opposite direction.

Slade whirled in the saddle to face the front. Charging toward him was a group of three riders that had bulged around the bend beyond the straight stretch of trail. They were less than five hundred yards distant.

Slade glanced toward the bay. No good! He would be a settin' duck. He whirled Shadow to the left and sent him charging into the thorny growth. Shadow didn't like it but knew what was expected of him; he plowed ahead, snorting and blowing. Slade tried to shield his face with his arm as the thorns raked and the branches lashed him. It was darn tough going for both. And very quickly he heard shouts to the left and right. The drygulchers were converging on him from two sides and would be within easy shooting distance when he reached the open crest of the rise.

To halt and try and make a stand would be futile; he would swiftly be surrounded. He was on a darn hot spot and he knew it.

'And it's apt to get a lot hotter mighty fast,' he muttered as the shouts and the crashing steadily drew closer.

Suddenly he had an inspiration: hot— hotter! There was a strong wind blowing from the north. He jerked Shadow to a halt, swung from the saddle and with frantic speed pawed a big heap of fallen leaves together. They were so dry they crumbled under his hands. And the growth was also tinder dry, there having been no rain for many days.

Fumbling a match, he struck it and touched it to the leaves. They smoldered, flickered. He sprang back as a wall of flame roared up, licking the twigs and branches, which also caught instantly. In a moment the fire was billowing right and left and storming down the slope under the beat of the wind.

The crashing in the brush, which had been swiftly drawing nearer, abruptly ceased and was replaced by a torrent of alarmed yells and cursing. It resumed, going away from there in a hurry. Slade sped to his snorting horse, mounted and sent him racing up the steep slope. Despite the force of the wind from the north, the fire, creating its own fierce updraft, was rushing up the slope, too. The crashing below was now hardly audible above the bellow of the flames.

'And I'll bet some of those drygulching gents are going to be nicely scorched before they reach the trail,' he told the thoroughly disgusted Shadow.

Very quickly, though, he realized that he stood a darned good chance of getting well scorched himself. The fire was all around him, the heat becoming unbearable. Shadow squealed with anger as a burning branch, caught in an eddy of the wind, seared his rump. He bounded forward half his length and redoubled his efforts.

The thick, black smoke rolled in clouds. The flames leaped and crackled. Coughing, choking, Slade jerked his neckerchief over his nose and mouth, leaned forward in the saddle and urged the frenzied, laboring horse to greater speed. Began to look like he'd been too darn smart. He'd sent the drygulchers skalleyhooting, doubtless with crisped hides, but at the same time had possibly arranged matters so he'd take the 'big jump' himself, and in no very pleasant fashion.

Then, as death was gripping his throat with burning fingers, the growth began to thin. Another desperate effort by Shadow, his rider croaking encouragement through his cracked lips, and he was covering the last score of yards to the crest and comparatively clear air. Slade pulled him to a halt and he stood with legs widespread, head hanging, breathing in hoarse gasps.

Dismounting, Slade secured the canteen of water he always packed in his saddle pouch, bathed the horse's lips and gave him a drink from his cupped hands. Shadow sucked down several handfuls, rolled his eyes, snorted, shook the drops from his lips and raised his head. Slade made sure he had suffered no serious burns. Then he drank a little of the remaining water and gave Shadow the rest of it. After which he mopped some of the ash and black from his face, rolled and lighted a cigarette and felt much better.

'Well, thanks largely to you, horse, we put it over,' he said. 'I've a notion those hellions figured they'd caught the Devil by the tail. Anyhow, they got a fair premature taste of what our Mexican *amigos* speak of *as el infierno.* And if a horse happened to fall with one of them, that's right where *he* went.'

He finished his smoke, mechanically pinched out the butt, gazed at the smoldering and well-scorched growth below, from which plenty of smoke still rose, and mounted.

'We'll follow this hogback to where it ends, a couple of miles from town, and then hit the trail,' he decided. 'Take it easy; I don't think we've got anything more to worry about

97

today.'

How, he wondered as he rode, did the side-winders catch onto what he was doing and where he was to such an extent that they could set the trap they did. However, the answer was fairly obvious. Doubtless one of the ships he had observed on the bay, very likely the speeding tug, had relayed the word ahead to the band that came from the west, having previously alerted those from the east. Yes, that was probably the answer. A neat scheme that very nearly worked. Somebody had brains and the ability to instantly size up a situation correctly and take advantage of the opportunity it provided.

But what tug? He didn't have the answer to that one, either, and wished he had. It could have been any one of many. Aside from the Westport and Aransas outfits, there were several independent puffers at Corpus Christi, to say nothing of mavericks from Port Isabel, Brownsville, Port Lavaca and even one now and then from Galveston.

With a shrug of his shoulders he decided to let the matter rest for the moment and rode on, following the crest until the ridge finally petered out a couple of miles from town. The chaparral had already ended, a mile or so back. He descended cautiously to the trail. There was nobody in sight; he hadn't really thought there would be. Very likely the parboiled drygulchers had had enough of him for the time being.

Reaching town without further incident, he headed directly for the stable, where he assisted Sam, the keeper, to give the big black a good rubdown.

'Fire over to the west, wasn't there?' Sam asked. 'Saw a lot of smoke b'ilin' up over there.'

'Yep, and we very nearly got caught in it,' Slade replied.

'So I gather,' Sam observed dryly, giving him a searching look and then carefully examining a patch of scorched hair on Shadow's rump.'

'I got something upstairs that'll take care of that in a jiffy,' he said and stumped up the steps. Slade also examined the slight burn and shook his head.

'Bad enough to have to be all the time on the lookout for ground-running scorpions without having to put up with the water-traveling variety,' he growled disgustedly. 'Oh, well, makes things interesting.'

'If you'd caught a burning branch on your— hind quarters, you might not be so philosophical about it,' Shadow's answering snort seemed to say.

Slade washed up at the trough, smeared a little salve on his own burns and scratches, made sure Shadow had everything needful and started for the Matagorda and something to eat.

Abruptly he changed his mind and turned his steps to the Westport offices. Vera might not yet have had her lunch; she might be waiting for him to put in an appearance.

She was, and there was nobody in the outer office. She started up from behind her desk, began to voice a greeting, then abruptly ceased, staring at him.

'Good heavens! what happened to you?' she exclaimed. 'Your face is all scratched.'

'Got tangled up with a thicket,' he returned composedly. Vera eyed him with evident disbelief.

'All right, tell me what happened,' she demanded.

He told her everything, for he felt she had a right to know. She listened, wide-eyed, one hand pressed against her scarlet lips.

'They might have killed you!' she breathed.

'They didn't,' he replied cheerfully.

'But they tried to!'

'Guess that was the general idea, all right,' he admitted the obvious.

'Walt, has my—hiring you got you into this trouble?' she hesitated.

'Nope, little lady, it hasn't,' he replied. 'I was already in it before I first laid eyes on you.'

'How? Tell me,' she urged.

'I will,' he answered and proceeded to do so, starting from the beginning, which was the incident of Malcolm Henderson being killed and his body brought ashore by his murderers.

'So I am to blame, if indirectly,' she said when he finished.

'I can't see it that way,' he disagreed. 'And by hiring me, you provided me with a much better chance of bringing Henderson's murderers to justice.'

She regarded him in silence for a moment, then, 'Walt, just what are you?' she asked. 'I don't mean that claptrap about your being an outlaw. What really are you?'

Slade arrived at a decision. By taking her fully into his confidence, he believed he would better further his ends. From a cunningly concealed secret pocket in his broad leather belt he drew something and handed it to her—a gleaming silver star set on a silver circle, the feared and honored badge of the Texas Rangers.

She gazed at the badge, turned it over and over in her fingers and handed it back to him.

'I suppose I shouldn't be particularly surprised,' she said. 'You are typical of the Rangers. So at least you are not alone, against your enemies, as I feared you were.'

'Decidedly not,' he agreed. 'I have all the power and prestige of the great state of Texas back of me.'

'But you are constantly in danger.'

'Aren't we all, constantly?' he rejoined. 'Take the incident by the bay, when Henderson's body was brought ashore. Had I been but a chuckline riding cowhand I would have ended up exposed to the same danger, in the nature of being a witness to the crime. And had I been other than what I am, lack of experience in such matters might have caused me to make the wrong move and really have gotten myself killed. Anyhow, if our number isn't up, nobody can put it up.'

'Isn't that fatalistic?'

'Only to the extent that we are in the hands of the Power that sent us here for better or for worse. It is up to us to try and conserve our lives until He needs us elsewhere. If we live as we should live, I don't think He will allow our existence to be terminated until the proper time.'

'That is comforting,' she said. 'Without Faith, life wouldn't be worth much, would it?'

'And with Faith, life is a glorious adventure.'

'Yes!'

She smiled at him, although her big eyes were a trifle misty. Quickly, however, her naturally ebullient spirits gained the ascendancy and she laughed gaily.

'If I don't eat soon, I won't conserve *my* life,' she said. 'I'm starving to death waiting on you.'

'Let's go,' he replied. 'Tonight we'll have another talk. There are a few things I wish to ask you about. Meanwhile I'll be busy on the waterfront.'

'And please try and keep out of danger for a

change,' she pleaded. 'Oh, well, though, the seamen's wives have to put up with the same thing. When their men go out on a cruise, they never know for sure that they'll return.'

'A sweetheart in every port,' he commented smilingly. Vera tossed her curls.

'Or one at every ranchhouse,' she replied pointedly.

Slade chuckled and did not continue the discussion.

ELEVEN

They lingered over their meal at the Matagorda. Slade escorted her back to the office and then returned to the waterfront and hunted up Si Hawkins.

'Hmmm!' remarked the captain, glancing at his scratched and slightly blistered face. 'Looks like you've been to the wars.'

'Went for a ride and tangled with a mesquite patch,' Slade replied. Which was true.

'Must have been mighty hot mesquite,' Hawkins commented, gazing westward where streamers of smoke were still rising.

'I'll tell you about it later,' Slade chuckled. 'Right now I want to ask a few questions.'

'Shoot,' said the captain.

'The two Westport steamers here, just when

did they dock and where from?'

'The Rosita docked the morning you took charge, a few hours before you showed up,' Hawkins replied. 'She's in from Tecolutia, Mexico. The Albatross docked three nights ago, a bit after midnight. She should have dropped anchor before dark but she had crank trouble and had to heave to a few hours for repairs.'

Slade nodded thoughtfully. Three nights ago was the night Malcolm Henderson was murdered, and when the Ranger had noted the lights of a ship standing offshore.

'The Albatross is the ship I ordered cleaned up,' he remarked.

'That's right,' Hawkins agreed.

'What's her captain's name?' Slade asked.

'Vane—Howard Vane.'

'Has he been with the company long?'

'Several years,' Hawkins replied.

'He was acquainted with Malcolm Henderson, of course?'

'That's right,' Hawkins nodded. 'Him and Henderson were on good terms; used to drink together.'

'I see,' Slade said, even more thoughtfully. 'And I understand Henderson was also quite well acquainted with Del Gregory, the sheep owning cattleman.'

'That's right, and so was Vane. The three of them used to drink together; they were on good terms, always seemed to have a lot to talk about.'

'I see,' Slade repeated. He arrived at a decision.

'Si,' he said, 'I'd like to have another look at the Albatross.'

Together they mounted the gangplank to the deck. There they found the crew busy at a little more furbishing. Slade again noticed the faintly unpleasant odor that had offended his olfactory nerves before. Captain Vane came forward to meet them, smiling pleasantly.

'Captain,' Slade said, 'I'd like to have a look below decks.'

'Sartin,' the skipper responded cheerfully. He led the way to the main hatch. They descended the ladder and found themselves in Hold One. Here the odor was more pronounced and Slade instantly identified it.

'Sheep!' he muttered to himself. 'This tub has been packing sheep on this deck.'

A glance around confirmed his judgment. Lying against one bulkhead was a contraption of heavy planks that was undoubtedly a ramp which, when put in place, would provide a gentle descent to the second deck. He glanced around casually, peered down into the dark hold and complimented the captain on the condition of things. He had learned what he wanted to know, and which dovetailed with a theory he had developed while talking to Hawkins.

'You've got a nice craft here, now,' he told

the skipper. 'Keep her that way.'

'I will,' the captain promised. 'You won't find cause for further complaint, sir. Guess I was just a mite too easy with the boys.'

'Not hard to contract that habit with men who have been with you a long time; but give them too much leeway and they'll sometimes get out of hand. Be seeing you, Captain.'

When they regained the wharf, Slade asked Hawkins, 'Si, do the Westport ships ever pack sheep?' Hawkins shook his head.

'Nope,' he replied, 'that was one of old Mitch Allen's loco notions. He hated sheep, had no use for them and wouldn't put up with them in any form. Wouldn't even load sheep hides or dressed meat or wool. Said the devil with them; he didn't need sheep.'

Slade nodded with satisfaction; his theory was further substantiated. The antipathy of the oldtime cattleman for sheep often verged on the ridiculous. The present case was an example. Nonsense, yes, but it wasn't easy to make a stubborn old cowman see it that way.

'Money in loading sheep, too,' Hawkins remarked. 'They're easy to handle and the sheep raisers pay well to have them transported by water. They do smell up a ship to beat the devil, though. Guess that's one of the reasons lots of masters object to loading them. Old Mitch was right, in a way; he didn't want to take the chance of being boycotted by the cattle raisers—more of 'em than sheep raisers in this section. Right now, at least. The other owners sorta followed his lead, and some others wouldn't load the woolies.'

Slade nodded again, and asked another question, 'Si, where are the Aransas tugs? I don't see either of them around.'

'Headed west this morning, a little after you left,' Hawkins replied. 'Bound for Port Isabel, I believe. Understand they had contracted for something over there.'

Slade did not comment, but he had a notion the Aransas tugs did *not* plan to put in at Port Isabel. The second half of his theory was becoming less vague.

For a long moment he stood gazing westward. The case, he felt, was in a way the most peculiar with which he'd ever had to deal. But aside from certain out of the ordinary ramifications, the basic pattern was familiar enough—robbery and murder, the lust for gain. Well, at last he was beginning to get a glimmering of the truth. He hoped to learn more shortly.

The Rosita, the other Westport steamer, was loading cargo preparatory to sailing for Galveston. The Albatross would start loading the next day. Slade said 'so long' to Hawkins and walked slowly uptown to the Westport offices. He found Vera Allen at her desk.

'Perch that perky hat on your beautiful curls and come along,' he told her. 'We got things to do.'

'Anything you say, dear, as usual,' she replied. 'Okay, I'm ready.'

Slade led her straight to the Albatross. He beckoned Captain Vane, who came forward, smiling and bowing.

'Want to have a little conflab in your cabin,' Slade said. The skipper ushered them in. Slade closed the door. They sat down, the captain facing them and looking a bit apprehensive. Doubtless he wondered just what this unexpected visit by the owner meant and if it had to do with the condition in which Slade found his ship in the course of his tour of inspection. It was safe to say that he did not in the least expect the question the Ranger shot at him.

'Captain,' Slade said, 'Malcolm Henderson was on your ship the night he was killed, was he not?'

The skipper jumped in his chair and began to perspire; but doubtless the pale, cold eyes meeting his convinced him that it would be unwise to try to evade.

'Y-yes, he was,' he admitted. Slade nodded and glanced warningly at Vera, whose eyes had widened as she stared at the captain, her red lips slightly parted.

'And you were to put him ashore to meet Del Gregory?'

'That—that's right,' faltered the captain, who was now perspiring freely.

'Suppose you tell us just what happened, so

far as you know,' Slade suggested.

Captain Vane took a deep breath and plunged into the subject as a man plunges into icy water—best to get it over with in a hurry.

'We were steaming in just at dusk. We aimed to put Mr. Henderson ashore in one of the dinghys. But we saw a boat rowing out to meet us. We hove to and waited. There were five men in the boat, dressed like cowboys dress. They hailed us and told me Mr. Gregory had borrowed the boat and told them to row out and pick up Mr. Henderson. Didn't seem to be anything strange about the request and I figured they were some of Gregory's cowboys. So Henderson got ready and we lowered him to the boat. Those cowboy-looking fellows asked if one of our sailors would come along to help row the boat, that they were doing a poor job of it and were afraid they might capsize her. That sounded reasonable, too, so I said okay. They said they'd see to it that he reached Corpus Christi okay.'

'Then what?' Slade asked as Vane paused to mop his face.

'Then one of the deckhands stepped forward and volunteered for the job, a man I'd hired about a month before and who said he lived in Corpus Christi and would be glad of a chance to spend the night with his folks, which he wouldn't get a chance to do if he stayed with the ship till she docked. Sounded all right to me, so I told him to go ahead.'

'Can you tell me anything about him?' Slade asked.

'Not over much,' the skipper answered. 'He didn't know a great deal about the work, about as much as could be expected from a lubber who'd made a few trips up and down the Rio Grande, as he said he had. But he was willing and seemed eager to learn. Was always first to tackle a tough job. I formed a good opinion of him. And when he asked to take on the job of rowing the boat to shore so he could spend the night in Corpus Christi, I was glad to do him the favor.'

'And you haven't seen him since,' Slade stated rather than asked. The captain shot him a bewildered look.

'That's so,' he admitted, 'I haven't. Figured he had a row with his wife and went off on a big drunk, just like anybody would do.'

Slade shot a glance at Vera, who bit her lip and made a face at him.

'Go ahead with your yarn, Captain,' he directed.

'That fellow took one of the oars and the boat pulled away,' Vane continued. 'By that time it was dark, a mighty dark night you may remember. We were upping the anchor and making ready to sail for Corpus Christi when we heard a cry somewhere out on the water. Thought maybe those cowboy lubbers had capsized the boat. Cry wasn't repeated,

110

though. We were just getting under way when we heard a lot of shooting over on the shore. Didn't know what was happening but figured we'd do well to get away from there. We did.'

'Not a bad idea,' Slade conceded. His eyes bored into the uncomfortable mariner's. He spoke, 'And Henderson was carrying the money he got for the sale of Gregory's sheep in Port Lavaca, was he not?'

Again the captain jumped in his chair, and this time he really jumped. Slade thought for a moment he was going through the cabin ceiling.

'So you know about that, too!' he groaned. 'Guess I'm finished with this Line.'

For the first time since beginning his interrogation, Slade smiled, and the little devils of laughter danced in his eyes.

'Oh, no you're not,' he said. 'Your intentions were good, even though your methods were a mite unorthodox, as I'm sure Miss Allen will agree when she gets the drift of things. Go ahead.'

'Yes, he had the money, in a satchel,' the captain said, looking greatly relieved. 'When we got to Corpus Christi and learned what had happened to Henderson, we got together and agreed the best thing we could do was keep our mouths shut until we learned more about what really happened. Aside from that swab I told you of, my boys have been with me a long time and I knew I could trust them not to talk.'

'A wise decision, circumstances being what they were,' Slade agreed.

Vera spoke for the first time. 'But why all the secrecy about the sheep cargo, Captain?'

'Well,' said the captain, again looking uncomfortable, 'it was this way. Your uncle had no use for sheep, didn't want to handle them or have anything to do with them. Mr. Henderson didn't feel that way. He thought your uncle's attitude toward sheep shipments was nonsense. Your uncle relied on him and he'd been taking over the management of the Line more and more. Your uncle was very old and not the man he once was. Henderson knew the Line hadn't been showing the profit it should because of lack of efficient managership. He knew there was good money from handling sheep. He and Del Gregory had been getting very friendly and when Gregory wanted to ship to Port Lavaca, Henderson thought it was a good notion. He knew he could slide the cargo money into his accounts without your uncle knowing where it came from. That was what he did with another shipment. Everything was going along smoothly and then your uncle died and you took over. We didn't know how you might feel about sheep and figured it was best to keep quiet, go through with what had already been contracted for and try and find out how you did feel about it. Reckon we should have told you first off. We meant for the best, though.'

'I assure you, Captain, that I have no objections to sheep,' Vera replied. 'If Mr. Gregory wishes to ship sheep by way of the Westport vessels, we will be glad to get the business.'

'That's where you're smart,' Slade interpolated. 'It's only a matter of time until sheep largely replace cattle in this section, and for quite a while. When a man like Dick King runs in forty thousand head, the handwriting is on the wall.'

'That's the way I feel about it,' Vera said. 'After all, I'm of a different generation from my uncle. You can't stop progress in any form, and it's foolish to try.'

'Right,' Slade said. He stood up. 'Well, guess that's all.'

'And much obliged, sir, for everything,' said the captain. 'I feel a lot better with it off my chest.'

'And thank you, Captain,' he replied. 'The information you gave us may help greatly to bring Henderson's killers to justice. Hope you have a pleasant voyage. Understand you head for Vera Cruz as soon as you load cargo.'

'We'll get at it early in the morning, hope to sail by dark,' the skipper said.

'I'll see you tomorrow,' Slade promised. 'Now I've got to see how the Rosita is making out with her cargo.'

113

When they reached the wharf, Vera said, 'What a weird story!'

'Yes,' he agreed. 'Deceit, even with the best intentions, has a habit of backfiring, as it did with poor Henderson. That deckhand the skipper spoke of, he was planted aboard the ship, of course. Evidently they loaded the sheep over to the east of here, near Gregory's spread. Deep water over there, so they could put in to shore and run the woolies aboard. Somebody caught on and planted that hellion to get information. He learned that Henderson was going with the shipment to dispose of the sheep and bring back the money paid for them to Gregory. So they set a trap and sprang it successfully.'

'Walt,' she said, 'I think I should reimburse Mr. Gregory for his loss. After all, the money was entrusted to one of my employees.'

'A nice gesture on your part,' he applauded. 'I doubt if the sum is overly large.'

'The Company can stand it,' she replied. 'And it'll make me feel better. Will you handle it for me, dear, contact Mr. Gregory and so forth?'

'Yes, I'll handle it,' he agreed. 'Wouldn't be surprised if Gregory is in town tonight. I heard it's payday for the spreads hereabouts and the boys will be in for a bust.'

She nodded and was silent for a few minutes as they walked back to the office.

'Walt,' she said, 'do you know who killed

114

Henderson?'

'I have a hazy notion, not one I'm ready to talk about yet, for I could be wrong,' he answered. 'There's something very strange going on in this section. The murder and robbery of Henderson was just an incident. I have an idea who is responsible for all the heck raising hereabouts, but just how it's worked I don't yet know. Well, we'll see; maybe I'll get a break.'

'And if you do bring the criminals to justice, I suppose you'll be leaving?' she said slowly.

'I'll promise you this much,' he said. 'If necessary I'll get a leave of absence and stay on until everything is running smoothly for you.'

'And then?'

'By then you may have changed your mind,' he replied smilingly.

'I won't!'

'Then we'll see.'

She sighed, but did not press him further.

They reached the office and Slade said, 'Now I'll have to be getting back to see how the Rosita is making out with her loading.'

'You'll take me to dinner tonight, of course. And—'

'Of course,' he laughed. 'I have to do something to earn my pay.'

'Tramp!'

TWELVE

Back at the wharf, Slade was satisfied with the progress being made. He was also fairly well satisfied with the day's developments. He felt that he had accomplished something. He had at least solved one angle of the mystery. But the more important problems still confronted him. He did not know who killed Malcolm Henderson. He did not know who tried to drygulch him. Nor did he know who nearly wrecked the steamer that straddled the reef. And until he had the answer to those questions, his task was far from finished. He had a notion who might well be the guilty parties, but you can't take a notion into court.

Si Hawkins strolled over to join him. 'Well,' he said, 'did the Big Boss give Skipper Vane a wigging?'

'Nope,' Slade replied. 'She complimented him on the condition of his ship.'

'She's all right,' Hawkins nodded. 'The boys are all for her after what happened by the Matagorda the other night. Seem to have forgotten all about her being a woman. They're proud to be sailing under her orders.'

'And I predict they'll continue to be proud,' Slade replied. Hawkins nodded emphatic agreement.

Hawkins glanced across at the Water Street

saloons. Already a number of cow ponies were tethered at the racks.

'The cowhands are drifting in,' he said. 'The places will be booming tonight. The payday bust. Going to bring Miss Allen down?'

'Sure,' Slade replied. 'We're going to have dinner here.' He glanced at the sunset sky. 'I'll be going after her in an hour or so.'

*   *   *

When Slade and Vera entered the Matagorda, a couple of hours later, the place was already beginning to hum and was well crowded. However, the proprietor, twirling his mustache, met them at the door with a low bow.

'I saved a table for you,' he announced proudly. 'Felt sure you and Miss Allen would join us tonight. Come right along, in the corner by the dance-floor, from where you can see everything. Liable to be some lively doings before the night is over. We seldom have any bad trouble here, though; the boys just get sorta kittenish now and then.'

'But kittens have claws,' Slade said, with a smile. 'And sometimes they use them. Thank you, Bert, for reserving the table for us; we both appreciate it, for we're hungry.'

'I'm starved,' Vera put in. 'He keeps me waiting till all hours.'

117

'Soon take care of that,' Bert declared energetically. He beckoned a waiter and headed for the kitchen to supervise the preparation of their meal.

They had finished eating and were enjoying a bottle of wine Bert had insisted they partake of when Vera suddenly exclaimed, 'There he comes, now.'

Slade had already noted the entrance of Del Gregory, with him his range boss and half a dozen of his hands. They found places at the bar and ordered drinks. Slade waited a little while, then caught Gregory's eyes and beckoned him to join them.

Gregory came over and diffidently occupied the chair Slade gestured him to. He glanced at Vera, a trifle apprehensively.

'Conscience makes cowards of us all,' Slade murmured to himself. 'He's scared, with no really good reason for being so.' He decided to have a little fun with Mr. Gregory.

'Del,' he asked, without preamble, 'just how much was your loss when the money paid for your sheep at Port Lavaca was stolen from Malcolm Henderson the night he was killed?'

Gregory jumped in his chair and began to perspire, just as Captain Vane of the Albatross had done.

'Wha-wha-what!' he gasped.

'I tried to, speak plainly,' Slade replied. 'Just how much did you lose? You see, Miss Allen feels that her Company should reimburse you for your loss.'

'B-but I don't see how she could be held responsible,' Gregory protested, looking dazed. 'The arrangement was made without her knowledge.'

'Perhaps not legally, but that's the way she feels about it, and you can't argue with a lady. Just how much did you lose?'

Gregory hesitated, then named the amount.

'Walt will hand you a check for it tomorrow,' Vera put in.

'Ma'am, I'm really much obliged,' Gregory said. He grinned, a trifle sheepishly. 'I'll have to admit it hit me sorta hard.'

'You'll get your check tomorrow,' Vera repeated. 'I suppose you'll be here tomorrow?'

'I certainly will,' he agreed, with alacrity. He shook his head in bewilderment.

'And you know all about it, I mean my arrangement with Henderson, who thought it was in the best interests of your company,' he marveled.

'Yes, we know all about it,' Slade replied. 'And why it was done. It would have been better for Henderson, and everybody else, though, if he had confided in Miss Allen.'

'Yes, I reckon it would,' Gregory sighed. 'But, you see, I'd already made commitments, and we didn't know for sure but that she'd share her uncle's dislike for sheep. So we decided to go through with it and keep quiet, and not do it again.'

Slade smiled. 'I think I can presume to assure you that the Westport Company will be glad to handle any future shipments you may feel inclined to entrust to it.' Vera nodded agreement.

'I'll have another flock ready before long,' Gregory said, his eyes brightening.

'The Albatross will run them to Port Lavaca when she returns from her voyage to Santa Cruz,' Slade promised.

'It'll sure help me a lot,' Gregory said gratefully. 'I sell to a packing house over there.'

'Poor sheep!' Vera said.

'Oh, the sheep don't mind,' Slade assured her. 'They know what their destiny is and that they are sacrificed in a good cause.'

'I'd have to have a sheep's word as to that,' Vera replied dryly. 'But they're doomed anyhow, so I don't see how we can be blamed for sending them in comfort on their way.'

'Then it's a deal,' Slade said to Gregory. 'Only we're liable to charge you a little more for disinfectant to rid the ship of that blasted smell.'

'I have a preparation that'll do the trick,' Gregory replied.

'Attar of Roses, perhaps?' Vera murmured. Slade wrinkled his nose.

'What a combination! Gives me the creeps just to think about it.'

They laughed together, then Gregory said,

with a boyish smile, 'Ma'am, I hope you won't mind me saying it,' he said, 'but gold is just plain dirt alongside you folks!'

After paying the compliment, one of the cowboy's highest, he departed hurriedly for the bar where he engaged his hands in conversation. A moment later the group turned as one man to face the table, and raised their hats. Slade stood up and acknowledged the courtesy with a wave of his hand.

'He's nice,' said Vera, apropos of Gregory. 'I'm glad to be able to lend him a helping hand.'

'Yes, and he's up-and-coming,' Slade said. 'I expect that, from a strictly business point of view, lending him a hand will pay off big. After all, men like Dick King and Shanghai Pierce and John Chisum started out with little or nothing. Gregory is liable to end up in their category. And I don't think he's the sort that forgets.'

'I hadn't thought of it in that light, but no doubt you are right,' she replied. 'It seems you always are.'

'Not always, I fear,' he deprecated. 'Nice of you to say it, but most of us do more foolish things than wise ones, and I sometimes think I am exceptionally cursed in that respect. When I look back on my past, I can scarcely see the scanty flowers of wisdom that decorate its path because of the fat, ugly trees of error by which it is overshadowed.'

'In the first place,' she disagreed, 'your past can hardly be called a long one—you're not so terribly much older than myself. In the second place, I'm judging from personal experience and from what others say of you, including such men as Sheriff Davis, Mack Russell, and Captain Hawkins. They can't all be wrong, and in fact I think none of them are. So there!'

Slade chuckled, and gave up the argument.

'Say, this joint is beginning to really hop,' he changed the subject.

It was. The bar was crowded three deep. The roulette wheels spun so fast they smoked. There were a number of poker games under way and the quietness of the players indicated the stakes were rather high. The faro bank was going strong. On the dance-floor the couples barely had room to shuffle. But the sailors and the cowhands just held the girls tighter, and the girls didn't seem to mind. The orchestra strummed and fiddled madly and there were bursts of song. Smoke eddied and whirled, from the sawdust rose the tang of spilled whiskey. Altogether it was a hilarious payday night. So far, just good clean fun, but Slade knew that after the redeye started buzzing in ears, most anything was liable to happen. He glanced at his table companion a bit doubtfully, then bit back a grin.

Vera's eyes were sparkling, her cheeks were flushed, her red lips slightly parted. There was no doubt but she was thoroughly enjoying herself.

'I love it,' she answered the question he put to her. 'I've been pretty well cooped up for the past month, and it was getting darned monotonous. This is really living.'

'Wait till a grand row starts, as one is likely to before the night is over, then we'll see how you like it.'

'Huh! I'd like it still more,' she retorted. 'Don't think you can scare me, my darling. After all, I was brought up on a ranch and in a Gulf town and have experienced some stirring times.'

'Flying lead and thrown bottles don't play favorites,' he warned.

'I can duck,' she replied complacently. 'This is a nice heavy table. Under it one should be fairly safe. But if a row starts, you stay out of it. You're here to look after me tonight, not to get mixed up in ruckuses, as the boys say. Asking a lot of you, though, I suppose. I think it hurts you to see a fight and not be able to get into it.'

'Most fights in such places as this are private fights and you're not supposed to horn in without an invitation,' he answered.

'Okay, then wait for one,' she said. 'Yes, I'll have another glass of wine, and if we can squeeze in, after a while, I want to dance.'

'You don't take up much room,' he reassured her.

'Oh, there's enough of me.'

'Without a single doubt,' he agreed, with emphasis. Vera dimpled, blushed, and made a face at him.

More and more seamen and cowhands kept crowding into the Matagorda, which was evidently favored by both. There were shopkeepers and office workers also, and Vera was not the only lady in the place. Several of the cowboys and quite a few of the sailors had their girls with them, and all appeared to be having a good time.

'There's Mr. Watson Payne, who owns a ranch and the Aransas Salvage and Shipping Company,' Vera suddenly remarked.

Slade nodded. He had already watched the big powerfully built Payne enter and glance around. He made his way to the bar, where several of the Aransas deckhands Slade recalled were grouped, said a few words to them and moved a little aside.

'Who's the big rough looking gent glowering at Payne as if he didn't like him?' Slade asked his companion.

'That's Captain Angus McClosky,' Vera replied. 'He owns a couple of tugs and a small steamer. He and Mr. Payne don't get along, I understand. I heard Captain McClosky accused Mr. Payne of undercutting his rates and taking business away from him. I don't know whether it's true.'

Recalling certain incidents relative to the

actions of the Aransas Company, Slade was inclined to believe it was. Vera had never mentioned Watson Payne's name, but he remembered that Sheriff Davis had remarked that there was rivalry between the Westport and the Aransas Company that almost amounted to bad blood. That was when old Mitch Allen headed the Westport Company, though. Or so he had understood the sheriff to indicate. Anyhow, it appeared Payne was a hard man to buck in a business deal. He watched the two men closely, for they were now tossing remarks back and forth.

It happened! Suddenly McClosky let out a bellow of wrath and swung a blow at Payne's face. The rancher ducked and the fist whizzed over his shoulder. His own hand shot out and down. Slade heard a crunch of steel on bone and McClosky fell to the floor senseless, blood pouring from his split scalp.

The Aransas men surged in behind their boss. Another group uttered angry cries. For a moment it looked like a real shindig. But Bert, the owner, was there, and his floor men, shouldering between the two groups with admonishing words. Almost instantly they were reinforced by several waiters, all ready for business.

Payne cast a contemptuous glance around and shrugged his heavy shoulders. He jerked his hand down, twisting his wrist, and turned back to the bar. McClosky was packed to the back room to get patched up. The two groups glowered at each other, but there were no further hostilities.

'Good heavens! what did he hit him with?' Vera asked. 'Captain McClosky went down like a pole-axed steer.'

'A gun,' Slade replied laconically.

'A gun! I didn't see him draw a gun.'

'Doubtless very few others saw it, either, but he drew one, all right,' Slade answered. 'What you just saw, my dear, was what's known as the gambler's draw.'

'The gambler's draw?'

'Yes. It's a hard one to master, but it is fast, and highly efficient. A stubby, double-barreled derringer, usually Forty-one calibre, is cached in a sleeve holster. With a forward thrust of his hand, a man who knows how can slide the derringer from his sleeve into his palm and be all ready for business. Makes a very good club, too, as you may have noticed.'

'Why is it called the gambler's draw?' she asked.

'Because it's one often employed by gamblers, especially professional card dealers. It has an advantage. A man can make the draw as swiftly and efficiently when sitting as when standing, and dealers are usually sitting when they need to resort to an iron.'

Vera shuddered. 'It wasn't a nice thing Mr. Payne did,' she said. 'He might have killed Captain McClosky.'

'Yes, he might have,' Slade conceded. 'Apparently, though, he decided not to.'

'You mean he *could* have killed him?'

'Well,' Slade returned dryly, 'suppose he had pulled both triggers instead of clubbing McClosky?'

Vera made a wry face. 'I said a little while ago that I wouldn't mind seeing a row, but that one left a bad taste in my mouth,' she replied.

Slade was silent, for he admitted to himself that the incident had affected him much the same way. Payne's act had been so cold-bloodedly impersonal. He regarded the ranch and ship owner with interest, and his black brows drew together in thought.

The affair at the bar had been so sudden and so quickly controlled that it made hardly a ripple and already the crowd had apparently forgotten all about it. Which was not remarkable. The drinks were strong. The cards behaved in their usual tantalizing manner that evoked muttered curses from the players. The dice skipped across the green cloth like spotty-eyed devils. The roulette wheels whirred cheerfully. The music was exhilirating, the eyes of the girls were bright. So why pay a ruckus any mind; next one might be livelier and more interesting. Powder River! I'm an old he-wolf from Bitter Creek and it's my night to howl!

Slade gazed at the open windows that faced to the south and arrived at a sudden decision.

'Listen, honey,' he said, 'I'm going to have a look outside and then speak to Captain Hawkins a minute; I'll be right back.'

'Now don't go getting into something,' she cautioned. 'Remember, you said it was a private fight.'

'I won't,' he promised. 'I'll be right back.'

He made his way through the crowd and out the door to the street, drawing a deep breath of the clean night air that had a salty tang. Just as he thought, the wind was rising, and it was coming from the southeast. Overhead, patches of cloud were hurrying past. The bay had a restless sound. He gazed across the troubled waters for a moment, then returned to the saloon and drew Hawkins aside.

'Si,' he said, 'Westport Three is patrolling over to the west, is it not?'

'That's right, per your orders,' returned the captain. Slade nodded.

'And as soon after daylight as you can get your crew together, you head over west, too. Try and stay within sight of the shore and keep a sharp eye out.'

'You figure something might happen over there?' Hawkins asked, looking puzzled.

'I don't know,' Slade admitted frankly. 'I'm

just playing a hunch, with nothing much on which to base it. I've just got a feeling.'

'I've a notion your hunches, as you call them, usually pay off,' Hawkins replied. 'Okay, I'll be steaming out with the dawn. Be seeing you.'

Returning to Vera, Slade sat down and rolled a cigarette. She glanced at him expectantly.

He repeated his conversation with Hawkins. She listened intently, a wrinkle between her delicate black brows.

'And you really think something might be going on out on the bay?' she asked.

'I don't know,' he replied as he had replied to Hawkins. 'I've just got a feeling that something might.'

He did not mention that he had noted that the Aransas seamen had, unobtrusively, slipped out, one by one. And even as he spoke, Watson Payne also sauntered out. He did not mention it because to do so would intimate something of which he was not at all sure. As he said, he was just playing a hunch; but as usual his 'hunch' was foundationed on a careful observance of facts and what they might contain. He had not an iota of proof that the Aransas Company was engaged in something off-color; he was just putting two and two together and making considerably more than four. Also, he had not failed to notice that Captain Bledsoe, with whom he had the ruckus by the reef to the west was conspicuous by his absence. Conjecture, nothing more, but his Ranger training had taught him not to ignore anything that did not admit of a plausible explanation. If his hunch paid off, he might be well on his way to solving the problem that confronted him. Anyhow, he wasn't going to miss any chances.

'Let's dance,' Vera suggested. 'The floor isn't quite so crowded anymore.'

'What difference does that make?' he said as they stood up. 'If it's crowded, it just gives me a chance to hold you closer.'

'I don't think you could any tighter than— come on, let's dance!' she replied, the dimple showing.

They had a couple of dances together, then Vera said, 'Walt, I think we should be going; it's past midnight and I've a notion you have a busy day ahead of you.'

'Could be,' he admitted, 'I'm ready if you are. Did I hold you close enough?'

'Not yet,' she giggled. 'Let's go!'

THIRTEEN

When Slade arrived at the waterfront the next day, the sky was overcast, the clouds rolling from the south-east, and the wind had definitely strengthened. Began to look a little as if a Gulf storm was in the offing.

He was rather surprised to see the two Aransas tugs lying in their slips. There was no sign of life aboard them, although the sun was well up in the sky. Evidently the crews were still sleeping after a busy night. Began to look like his hunch wasn't a straight one, after all.

The two tugs were still quiescent so far as human activities were concerned when Westport One, Captain Hawkins' tug, came booming into port. The captain waved to Slade, and as soon as his vessel docked and the gangplank was lowered, he came hurrying down to join him. His eyes were snapping with excitement.

'There's a ship over to the west about two hours' run from here,' he said. 'Looks like she's abandoned; we couldn't see a sign of anybody aboard her. She's low in the water and listing badly to starboard. I'd say she's got a lot of water in her, and maybe her cargo has shifted. She's the Albemarle, one of the Grayson Line's craft. Don't know what her cargo is, but I happen to know the Grayson people have contracts for loading machinery. Could be a mighty valuable manifest.'

Slade did some very fast thinking. 'Where's Westport Three?' he asked.

'She's standing by,' Hawkins replied. 'Figure to make a try for the Albemarle? She'll need a tow, if nothing more; but I'm willing to bet that for some reason or other the crew abandoned ship. Maybe because it looks like a bad blow is coming and ain't far off.'

'Yes we'll make a try for her,' Slade said. 'Wait a minute, though. Get the crew over here where I can speak to them.'

Hawkins did so and Slade addressed the seamen.

'Looks like a nice chore of salvage out there,' he told them. 'But also looks like a mighty bad blow is coming, and you know what that can mean in one of these tubs out on the open bay. Are you fellows willing to take a chance? I won't order anybody to go with me, but I'm open for volunteers.'

'Let's go, Admiral, let's go!' a chorus of voices answered. 'Full steam ahead!'

'Okay, and thank you,' Slade called back. 'How soon can you get under way?' he asked Hawkins.

'Soon as we refuel a mite,' the captain replied.

'I'll be with you by the time you're ready to shove off,' Slade promised and headed uptown at a fast pace. Now he was really playing his hunch.

Arriving at the stable where he kept Shadow, he quickly secured his Winchester. He paused to bestow a pat on the big black.

'Not this time, feller,' he said. 'Your fins haven't grown long enough yet for this sashay. Be seeing you!' He hurried back to the waterfront, where he found all in readiness to shove off.

Hawkins glanced curiously at the rifle. 'Taking that along?' he asked. 'Why?'

'Playing a hunch,' Slade replied, and did not elaborate. 'Say, it looks like the Aransas tugs have been tied up here all night,' he remarked.

'They haven't,' Hawkins differed. 'When I left the Matagorda, a bit after midnight, they weren't here. I didn't go to bed last night, and just before daybreak I saw them slide in. Then it 'peared the crew went to sleep. Didn't come ashore. Wonder where they'd been?'

'I wonder?' Slade rejoined, thoughtfully.

The tug got under way, and headed for the open bay under forced draft. Glancing back, Slade saw a man leaning over the rail of one of the Aransas tugs, apparently following their progress with his gaze. Abruptly he ducked back out of sight. The next minute the swirling mist wrack and the spray hid the Aransas craft from view.

Overhead the clouds had thickened and were taking on a slaty appearance. The gray waters of the bay were heaving now, the wind greatly increased in violence. Looked like a real ripsnorter was building up. Slade wondered if he had done the right thing in risking the tug's crew out on the wild water. She was a staunch little craft and accustomed to taking batterings, but there was a limit, and sometimes Corpus Christi Bay went a long ways past the limit, even for a larger and more seaworthy vessel than the Westport One. Well, Hawkins was undoubtedly an able and experienced skipper and his deckhands were mostly old-timers who had dared more than one puddle in a storm. Slade set his face to the roaring wind and hoped for the best.

Once well away from land, the tug veered sharply west, her funnel thundering, her screw lashing the water, the engine racing at times as the heave and surge of the laboring vessel jerked the propellor above the surface. She was wallowing a bit now, but making good headway. Overhead the wind was acquiring the hollow roar that hinted at a splitting apart of the envelope of the universe. Slade had heard that sound before and knew it presaged no good to come. But Westport One boomed on, ignoring the fury of wind and water and those steadily heightening waves rushing in endless succession from the dark southeast.

'Sorta growly, ain't she, eh?' bellowed Hawkins at his elbow. 'But this ain't nothing. Just wait till we're lashed to that blasted waterlogged steamer and beating back against wind and water.'

'Prefer to turn back now?' Slade asked.

'Blankety-blank it, no!' bawled the skipper. 'For this puff of wind and puddle of water? Down off old Cape Stiff this would be considered just a spring zephyr over a mill pond. Now we've started we're going through with it even if we all end up in Davy Jones' locker. Right?'

'Right!' Slade shouted back over the howl of the wind.

The tug surged on, plunging and wallowing, with the wind growing stronger, the sea rougher. The helmsman fought the wheel to the accompaniment of vivid profanity, Captain Hawkins lending a hand now and then as the spokes threatened to escape from his grasp. The crew hunkered in the lee of the bulwark, smoking and chatting.

An hour passed, the better part of another. Slade stood swaying easily to the heave and pitch of the deck, gazing steadily ahead. As the second hour drew to a close he saw what he sought, a faint darkening against the lowering gray of the westward sky.

'Westport Three is still standing by,' he called to Hawkins. 'I can see her smoke.'

The skipper peered with puckered lids. 'Hanged if I can see anything but clouds and salt water,' he growled. 'Wait, I'll get my glasses.'

He dived into the cabin, reappeared a moment later with his binoculars, which he trained on the western horizon.

'Darned if you ain't right,' he grunted after a moment or two of probing. 'What kind of eyes have you got, anyhow?'

Shortly afterward, Slade could make out

the shape of the standing-by tug, and the shadowy bulk of the stricken freighter. Hawkins focused his glass on her.

'Looks just the same as she did when we were here before,' he muttered. 'If she's got a leak it's funny she hasn't taken more water, with the pounding she's been getting.'

Slade had a very good notion why she hadn't taken more water, but he refrained from saying so at the moment. He wanted to be certain, and to perhaps discover some corroborating proof.

Westport Three's whistle sounded a greeting. Westport One answered with a few irritable toots. Hawkins studied the freighter.

'I think we can make it aboard over the starboard rail, the way she's listing,' he announced. 'Careful, you lubbers, when you try it. Fall in between and you'll get smashed to a pulp.'

Slade studied the Albemarle a moment, then voiced a warning.

'Don't try it, Si,' he said. 'She's rolling pretty heavily and you're liable to have your plates stove in if she really slams you one. Better to lower the dory and we can spring and make it to the rail when she rolls to starboard.'

'I expect you're right,' Hawkins conceded. 'We'll do it that way.'

As they drew near the freighter, which looked mighty big compared to the bug-like tugs, Westport One stood off and lowered the dory with its flat bottom and flaring sides. With two men at the oars, Slade, Hawkins and two deckhands took their place in the boat, which ran in close to the freighter's starboard.

Slade was first to go. He balanced himself on the thwarts, swaying easily to the tossing of the boat, and waited until the Albemarle rolled. The steel side looked monstrous as it rushed down toward him. He gaged the distance and as the ship completed the roll and before she could surge up again, sprang lightly and gripped the rail with his hands. Over it he went and onto the slanting deck.

Hawkins was next, coming over easily with the deftness of long experience. The deckhands followed, reaching the deck without mishap.

'A lot easier than out on the Atlantic or even the Gulf,' Slade remarked. 'Out there, a salvage job in bad weather is something to reckon with.'

'You're darn right,' Hawkins grunted agreement. 'Let's see, now, I think we can handle her by way of the bitts. If she was a mite bigger and heavier, we'd have to cut or burn through the anchor chain and splice onto that. With the chain running over the bows there would be less chance of the tow line parting.'

'Yes, I think we can risk the bitts,' Slade agreed. 'If we had a longer haul I'd say the chain, because the great weight of the chain tends to sag the towing line so there is less likelihood of it being stretched to the breaking point. The shape the Albemarle is in, I don't think we have to worry about that.'

'Right,' said Hawkins, and began bellowing orders. The tug backed cautiously to within fifty feet of the freighter's bow. A light heaving line was flung from the tug's afterdeck, which was deftly caught. Hauled aboard, it brought with it a manilla mooring line which in turn brought aboard the steel towing line.

It took the combined strength of all hands to get the towing line aboard and secured to the bitts, the fixed vertical metal castings set in the Albemarle's bow for securing hawsers, cables and other lines, such as the towing line in the present instance.

Hawkins rubbed his hands together complacently. 'We've got her,' he chuckled. 'Yep, she's our fish now. That is if the blasted line doesn't part, or something, or the sea doesn't get so rough it'll sink us both.

'It's liable to do just that, too,' he added, glancing apprehensively into the dark southeast. 'All right, everybody, off this tub, and onto the tug, where you'll be a heck of a sight safer if something does go wrong.' He waved the dory to stand in close. He and the deckhands lined up at the starboard rail, ready to drop into the dory. Slade held back.

Hawkins glanced at him inquiringly.

'I'm staying aboard,' he announced.

'You'll be taking a chance,' Hawkins protested. If that line happens to part, she's liable to go to the bottom before the storm's over.'

'I'll risk it,' Slade replied. 'Just throw up my rifle from the dory.'

Hawkins looked bewildered, but refrained from argument. The maneuver was successfully accomplished. Slade stayed on deck until the tow line tightened and the Albemarle began moving slowly in the wake of the laboring, wallowing tug. He had no doubt but the tug could handle her without difficulty —she had the power for the chore and would not need assistance from Westport Three, which kept pace.

Slade took a last look around to make sure all things were shipshape. The towing line was running smoothly over the chafing plate which minimized the danger of the line wearing and parting. The wheel was firmly lashed in place, to prevent the ship from veering.

Satisfied that everything was under control, he entered the captain's cabin and glanced around.

Everything appeared to be shipshape, with nothing disturbed. Not at all satisfied, however, he began a thorough examination of the cabin. Abruptly he paused beside the table bolted to the deck. In front of it was a similarly secured chair, where it should be, and on the wood of the table top was a dark stain.

Hanging on a nail driven into a bulkhead was a lantern. He secured it and touched a match to the wick. By its light he studied the stain, rubbing it hard with a fingertip and carefully examining the tip. Yes, there was no doubt about it—the stain was congealed blood that had not soaked into the wood.

'Just as I suspected,' he muttered aloud. 'Just as I suspected.'

He got down on hands and knees and examined the floor, and found a few more similar stains, smaller but the same.

Rising, he repaired to the forecastle, where the crew slept. There he found a certain amount of disorder. Some of the bunks had been stripped of sheets and blankets, which were nowhere in sight. Others showed no sign of recent occupancy, being neatly made. And on the floor he found more blood stains, faint but discernible to the eyes of El Halcón.

From nearby came a plaintive, 'Meooww!' Glancing around, he saw a whiskered face peering from under a bunk. 'Here, Puss!' he called, and the ship's cat emerged from hiding. It purred and rubbed against his leg.

More proof that the ship had not been willingly abandoned. The crew would never have left the cat aboard. To do so would be to risk incurring the worst of luck, from the sailor's viewpoint.

'I'll take care of you shortly, Puss,' he promised.

Taking the lantern with him, he went down into the holds for a look around. The cargo, heavy crates filled with machinery, had shifted some but not a great deal. At the foot of the ladder leading to Number Three he paused, listening to the swish and gurgle of water rising from the darkness below. The engine room and the coal bunkers were, of course, flooded.

Once again, just as he suspected. The sea-cocks had been opened long enough to allow the entrance of considerable water. To simulate an attempt to sink the vessel which for some reason had not been consummated. He turned back and ascended the ladders to the upper deck. His face was set in granite lines, his eyes were cold as the pale waters of a glacier lake.

His suspicions, and his hunch, had been justified. The ship had not been voluntarily abandoned. She had been attacked by 'pirates,' to stretch a point in nomenclature, her crew murdered, the bodies thrown overboard. The blood stained sheets and blankets of men killed in their sleep had also doubtless been thrown overboard; but the devils had neglected to carefully scrub away the blood stains on the table and the floor. The captain had been killed at his table, where he sat, perhaps going over his manifest. Yes, snake-blooded murder had been done aboard the Albemarle.

For what purpose? Slade was certain he had the answer to that, but he still had to prove it.

FOURTEEN

While he was below, the storm had increased in violence. The Albemarle was rolling and lurching, but the strain of the tow line kept her on a fairly even keel, considering the list to starboard. The big tug was wallowing but forging ahead steadily, Westport Three keeping pace with her to the left. He leaned against the forward bulwark and managed to roll and light a cigarette. His rifle lay at his feet. As soon as he finished the smoke, he'd go to the galley and break out a ration for the cat.

As he drew in deep and satisfying lungsful of the fragrant smoke, his eyes swept the tossing sea. Abruptly they focused on something coming up from the south. Something formless and shadowy in the murk. Quickly, however, it achieved form and substance and proved to be a big tug racing through the tossing seas under forced draft. He strained his eyes to read her name, and could not, realizing in another moment that it had been painted over or covered.

She appeared to be heading straight for Westport One. No! She would pass slightly astern of the Westport tug. Her purpose was obvious—to cut the tow line and set the Albermarle adrift! And now she was less than three hundred yards distant from the straining line. Slade could clearly make out the forms of the men on her deck, including the helmsman. He scooped up the Winchester and flung it to his shoulder; his eyes glanced along the sights. It was fair shooting distance for El Halcón, even from the heaving deck of a listing ship.

The rifle muzzle spurted smoke. The tug spun around crazily as the helmsman threw up his hands and fell. Slade's lips writhed in a mirthless grin.

Another man sprang to the wheel, steadied the careening tug, which was now less than a hundred yards from the tow line.

The rifle spoke again as the Ranger's pale, icy eyes lined sights. And again the tug whirled around out of control. Now she was almost opposite the Albemarle. Slade could almost hear the yells and curses as her crew dived wildly for shelter. He sprayed the deck with bullets, hoping to keep her out of control until she foundered.

But Hawkins, who had doubtless realized the danger, was sending Westport One plowing ahead with a wide-open throttle. The marauding tug fell behind and by the time

Slade had shoved fresh cartridges into the rifle magazine it was out of range and once more under control. He watched it steam northward like an elephant with a scorched tail, and caressed the Winchester affectionately.

'Mighty glad I brought you along, partner,' he told the gun. 'If I hadn't had you, it would very likely have been curtains for me. I've a prime notion the old tub would have capsized and sunk in this storm without the steadying influence of the tow line.'

On the two Westport tugs men were shouting and waving their arms, but their voices were but a reedy whisper of sound amid the turmoil of wind and water. Slade waved a reassuring hand in response and headed for the galley, where he uncovered a whack of cold meat for the cat, of which the feline mariner partook avidly. A good drink from a pan and it sat back contentedly washing its face with its paws.

Slade decided that the first half of its performance was worthy of emulation and proceeded to kindle a fire in the galley stove. Soon he had a pot of coffee bubbling.

The cold meat proved tasty and he made a very satisfying meal.

'If we're headed for Davy Jones' locker, as Captain Hawkins would say, we might as well make the trip on a full stomach,' he told the cat, adding a bit grimly, 'and if this old tub rolls to a little greater degree, that's very likely just what we'll do.'

After which, instead of washing his face with his paws, he rolled a cigarette and gave himself over to thought. After due consideration, he decided to take Captain Hawkins into his confidence, and Vera, of course. Otherwise he would hold his peace. It was not the time for what he had learned to become public knowledge. He felt it would be wise to show the old skipper the evidence of foul play he had discovered, and he was confident he would keep a tight *látigo* on his jaw.

'There'll be a lot of wild conjecture as to why the ship was abandoned and what became of the captain and the crew,' he told the cat. 'But let 'em conject, to coin a word. I wish you could tell me just what happened—you must have seen it—but I reckon you can't, unfortunately. It would simplify matters if you could. Well, anyhow, we did a hefty chore of salvage for the Westport Company. The cargo is worth plenty, and so is the ship. And I believe we're going to make it to port. The storm isn't behaving itself any better but we're in the lee of Mustang Island, which helps. Yes, I think we'll make it.

'And you're all set, too, cat,' he concluded. 'The Matagorda will give you a home and a good one. That is if Miss Allen doesn't decide to do so. Either way, you're on the top corral bar.'

After which he went out on the slanting, wind-swept deck. The cat stayed right where it was.

*　　　　*　　　　*

Slade's prediction was quite accurate. It was raining, but the wind had already greatly abated and the island broke the force of the waves. Westport One steamed cheerfully along, the tow line dipping and rising, the Albemarle ambling docilely in her wake like a contented cow on the end of a rope, with a helping of chuck in the offing. Hands waved from the tug and the Ranger waved back. Westport Three, convoying the tow, kept pace. Soon the two-tiered town of Corpus Christi came into view. Twenty minutes more and the two tugs were screaming jubilantly, their whistles sounding long blasts of triumph as they ploughed on through the choppy seas.

Westport One slowed her pace. Westport Three rushed forward to shove and nose the Albermarle to make her lose momentum. Slade freed the tow line for the tug to reel in. Followed a short period of careful maneuvering on the part of the tugs and the Albemarle was safely moored to the wharf. The tug whistles screamed again and were answered by every craft in the harbor, shouting aloud the word of another victory by man over the sea.

Now the waterfront was crowded by a cheering throng. When Slade went aboard, the cat in his arms, a little figure in oilskins darted ahead of everybody else.

'I've been frantic, absolutely frantic,' she sobbed, clinging to him. 'What's that? I don't care how much money you've made me! You'll be the death of me yet. You shouldn't have taken that awful risk. None of you should have. You should have stayed here when you knew that terrible storm was coming.'

'And leave this poor critter to drown or starve?' he said, stroking the cat, which purred loudly and kneaded its paws against his shirt front.

Tears and laughter are often close together, and she had to laugh at the aptness of his retort.

'Give it to me,' she said, 'it's getting wet. I'll put it under my oilskin.'

She proceeded to do so, leaving only a pink nose sticking out.

Captain Hawkins and his deckhands were gesturing toward Slade, and talking excitedly to men who shouldered each other to get close.

'Hurrah for the Admiral!' somebody shouted, and the cheers were given with a will.

To the sailors, especially the old deep-water men, it was a momentous event. Another saga of man's age-old warfare with the sea. Vera gave way a little as men crowded around Slade to congratulate him and shake his hand.

147

But she was back to him as soon as the press thinned out a lit. 'Come along,' she said. 'You're soaking wet. You need dry clothes.'

'And a rubdown,' he added seriously, but with the devils of laughter tumbling to the front of his cold eyes. 'Roses in the rain!' he chuckled, his gaze fixed on her glowing cheeks.

'Oh, come on and behave yourself,' she said, tugging at his sleeve. Tucking the Winchester under his arm, he gave in without further argument.

As they walked, he told her everything. Her breath caught in her throat as she listened without interruption.

'And if the tug had parted the tow line you would have drowned,' she said with startling accuracy when he paused.

'Well, she might have capsized,' he conceded.

'And you have no idea who owns that tug?'

'Her name was painted out or covered,' he temporized.

'But you have an idea,' she persisted.

'Yes, I have an idea,' he admitted. 'But I have no proof, because of which I prefer not to talk about it, yet.'

She did not press him further, but looked decidedly worried.

Slade's conversation with Captain Hawkins, later, followed much the same pattern.

'And who do you think she belongs to?'

148

asked the skipper.

'Whom do *you* think?' Slade evaded.

'Just about the same as you think, I reckon,' Hawkins answered.

'But until we get some proof, we are in no position to name names,' was El Halcón's rejoinder. Hawkins nodded sober agreement.

'Meanwhile you'd sure better watch your step,' he said. 'I've a notion they were more anxious to do for you than to sink the Albemarle. Oh, there was a good chance she would have capsized and sank; there would have been no getting another line on her, not with that wind and water. The murdering devils! I hope you finished off a couple of them. Sure was smart thinking on your part, taking the rifle along.'

'Playing a hunch,' Slade replied.

'A sorta good example of understatement, I'd say,' Hawkins returned dryly.

'And now we'll board the Albemarle,' Slade said. 'There's something I wish to show you.'

After a word with the two deckhands Hawkins had assigned to watch duty aboard the freighter, Slade led the way first to the captain's cabin. Hawkins' face froze in an expression of horror as the Ranger pointed out the evidence of a snake-blooded killing there and in the forecastle.

'It doesn't seem such devils could be allowed to live,' he marveled. 'Why, they're worse than the pirates of the old days were.'

149

'And smarter,' Slade commented.

'I wonder why they didn't drop a line on her and tow her in right away?' the skipper asked.

'Would have been a mite too obvious,' Slade explained. 'They preferred to play it the safer way and "discover" her later. They didn't count on two things, the rather unexpected storm and our patrols over to the west. Fortunately, they never caught on to that last or they would doubtless have made provisions against it. As it was we caught them flat-footed, and before they could get going we were a long jump ahead of them and had our line and our house flag aboard the Albemarle. Trying to cut the tow line with their tug was in the nature of a spite move; if they couldn't have her they figured to make sure we wouldn't either.'

'Uh-huh, and they didn't count on a crack shot aboard with a Winchester rifle,' Hawkins commented dryly. 'And that was another example of your smart thinking—having our tugs patrol those waters like you did. That gave us the advantage that paid off big.'

Slade figured he had not indulged in exaggeration when he expressed the opinion that these modern 'pirates' were smarter than those of other days. They did not loot and so could never be caught red-handed with their ill-gotten gains. Salvage was a legitimate enterprise. And the salvager was not supposed to concern himself with why the vessel was disabled or abandoned. His business was to, if humanly possible, get the casualty safely to port. There his obligation ended. If there had been something off-color, that was up to the proper authorities to deal with. He had performed his chore and was entitled to the customary recompense. In the case of the Albemarle, undoubtedly cold-blooded murder had been committed; but no witnesses had been left, aside from the cat, so far as Slade knew, and in such an incident it would be a very difficult matter to prove guilt against anyone. For the moment, to all appearances, he was up against a stone wall.

However, it was unlikely that there was ever such a thing as a perfect crime, especially when more than a single individual was involved.

Which was possibly the weak link in the chain; under the proper circumstances, somebody might be persuaded to talk. And there was always the chance that somebody would drop an incautious word.

FIFTEEN

That night he discussed the matter at length with Sheriff Berne Davis. As one lawman to another, he held back nothing, voicing his suspicions and the reasons for them.

'I'm confident,' he said, 'that Watson Payne and his Aransas outfit are the hellions responsible, but I'm hanged if I know how to prove it. Not yet, anyhow.'

The sheriff had been frankly dubious at first, but as Slade outlined the series of incidents he had noted, his doubt changed to amazed belief.

'I always figured Payne, though a tough business competitor, to be okay,' he said, shaking his head sadly. 'Seems you never can tell. Yes, it sure looks like they murdered the Albemarle's crew, all right.'

'That, of course, was the chore the Aransas tugs had in mind when they slipped out of port last night shortly after midnight,' Slade observed. 'They knew where to meet the Albemarle, boarded her and killed the captain and crew. Then they opened the sea-cocks and let some water into her. After which they steamed back to Corpus Christi and went to bed, planning to "discover" the stricken ship later in the day.

'It was clumsily handled, however,' he added. 'They'd have done better to leave the captain's body in the cabin, perhaps with a knife in the back. That would have made it look more like the crew had mutinied, killed the captain and then got frightened and abandoned ship. Their brand always slip up on the little details.'

'Uh-huh, if they're up against somebody

who doesn't slip where the little details, or any other sort are concerned,' remarked the sheriff. 'Well, I wouldn't want to be in their boots right now, with El Halcón hot on the trail.'

Slade smiled, a trifle wanly. 'Thanks for your confidence, but right now I feel sort of helpless,' he replied. 'I don't know which way to turn.'

'Think his riders are mixed up in this business?' the sheriff asked.

'I don't know for sure,' Slade admitted. 'Possibly but probably not. The men who brought Henderson's body ashore were or had been cowhands, of that I am pretty sure. And the two bunches that tried to drygulch me on the trail between here and the reefs where that steamer went aground certainly were. Also, there were signs of horses on the ground near the reef and the blocked channel. I didn't give it much thought at the time, surmising that the tracks were doubtless left by some riders drawn from the trail by curiosity after hearing about the steamer. But they could have been made by whoever blocked the channel with boulders.

'However, Payne may be, and very likely is, too smart to use his regular range riders for the chore. I've a notion the ranch, a small one I understand, is in the nature of a front, and lends an aura of respectability in a section like this.'

'He has a good standing in the community,' the sheriff interpolated.

'Exactly. And to also give him greater freedom of movement. Nobody would think anything of his riding around and scouting the bay, as very likely he does.' Slade paused to roll and light a cigarette.

'I wish I knew something of his background,' he resumed. 'I'm pretty sure that he has worked as a card dealer at times, probably on river boats and Gulf ships. Packing a sleeve gun and expertly manipulating the gambler's draw like he did last night when he walloped McClosky with his derringer tends to strengthen such an assumption. Dealing on boats and listening to stories told and things said by seamen may have provided the inspiration that got him into the salvage business. And once in it, he quickly realized the opportunities it offered for skullduggery.

'All that is merely surmise on my part, but with a certain amount of factual support.'

'I think you're plumb right on all counts,' said the sheriff. 'He's smart and ornery, all right, but there never was a horse that couldn't be rode.'

'Nor a man who couldn't be throwed,' Slade ungrammatically finished the couplet with a smile. The sheriff chuckled.

'Anyhow, now you know who to look for and who to look out for,' he said.

'Yes, and that helps a lot,' Slade answered. 'For a while I didn't know which way to turn. Then the steamer shunted onto the reef via the blocked channel sort of started me thinking in the right line. We got a break there. The owner of that launch was a friend of Captain Hawkins' and when he spotted the wreck he brought the word to Hawkins. The Aransas tug was all set and waiting for the word to be brought to them. They hightailed out but Hawkins was right behind them, and he had a bit of luck when the Aransas tug had steering gear trouble.'

'And when you showed up to tell him how to get the steamer off the rocks,' Davis put in. 'That sure riled Serge Bledsoe and got him a nice walloping.'

'Bledsoe may be a weak link in the chain,' Slade observed thoughtfully. 'He has an ungovernable temper that causes him to use bad judgment at times. I thought at the time it was a mite strange for him to get his bristles up so over what appeared to be nothing but a business matter. He figured that after they went to the trouble of bouncing her onto the reef, the salvage for the steamer belonged to them. He'd have done better to keep quiet once he saw he was licked.'

'But he didn't and let everybody *see* him get licked!' Davis chortled with glee at the remembrance.

'Catching onto Del Gregory's sheep deal

155

with Malcolm Henderson helped, too,' Slade continued. 'It showed me that somebody on the waterfront was keeping a close watch on everything that went on, which might provide opportunity for gain. Of course, I was already convinced, from previous reports, that somebody was wrecking ships with salvage in mind. The big question being who, and what outfit.

'Last night was the real payoff, though. Payne had learned of the Albemarle and the valuable cargo of machinery, and approximately where she should be between midnight and dawn. So he came to the Matagorda and told his crew and gave them orders to slide out one at a time, get their tugs under way and intercept the Albemarle. Which is just what they did. After doing their little chore of murder and, or at least they thought, making the Albemarle look like a ship abandoned by her crew, they sneaked back to port and went to sleep innocent as little woolly lambs, awaiting the order to steam out and "salvage" the Albemarle.

'So there's our case,' he concluded, 'hanging in the air with no foundation of proof to support it.'

'My money's still on El Halcón,' the sheriff declared sturdily.

'Hope you don't end up having to eat snowballs,' Slade smiled and rose to his feet.

'I'm going to call it a night,' he announced.

'Has been quite a day.'

'Quite a week, rather, and then some,' grunted Davis. 'And 'pears to be getting no better fast. See you tomorrow.'

Pretty well tired out, Slade slept rather late and awoke to a day of brilliant sunshine. After a leisurely breakfast he repaired to the waterfront to look things over. Westport One and Westport Three were fussing around a big Norwegian freighter that was shortly due to sail. He smiled thinly as he noticed that one of the Aransas tugs, which had been absent when Westport One steamed in with her tow, the Albemarle, was undergoing a thorough paint job, a number of her bow plates having been scraped.

Just coincidence, perhaps, but slightly significant in the light of the previous day's happenings. The Westport steamer, the Albatross, her chore of loading finished, was already well on her way to Vera Cruz.

The Albemarle had been pumped out and her shifted cargo was being put back in place. Slade went aboard for a while to watch the operation and was satisfied with the progress being made.

From the high deck, he could look down at the nearby Aransas tug that was being re-painted. He chuckled as he noticed that one of her wheel spokes was missing. Just coincidence again, perhaps, but a Forty-five slug fired from a high-powered rifle *did* have a habit of removing anything that got in its way.

After the Norwegian ship was nosed out, Captain Hawkins came ashore and joined Slade.

'Everything going smooth and easy,' he said. 'I saw Captain Serge Bledsoe a little while ago and he didn't look happy. Seems to me, too, that I counted a couple of faces that were with his crew the other night but ain't there now. Got a notion some of his swabs ain't feeling exactly shipshape, if they're able to feel at all.'

The skipper's remark was a bit hard to unscramble, but Slade got the point.

'I wouldn't be at all surprised,' he conceded. 'Well, I'm going up to the offices. Want to find out if there's any word from the Grayson Line. We wired them yesterday evening, acquainting them with what happened and that, we had the Albemarle safe in port. Be seeing you later.'

When Slade entered he found Vera at her desk. After greeting her, he sat down and rolled a cigarette.

'Hear from the Grayson people?' he asked.

'Their representative is on his way, by train,' she replied. 'He should arrive about seven o'clock. You'll be here, won't you?'

'Of course,' he assured her. 'Mind if I make a suggestion?' Vera smiled.

'You mean do I mind if you give me an order. What is it, dear?'

'Just this,' Slade answered. 'Don't hit the Grayson people for all you can get under the laws of salvage. A nominal sum will give you a handsome profit in addition to what the boys are entitled to. The Grayson people won't forget. They're big and will be able to throw a lot of business your way.'

'You're right, as usual,' she agreed. 'You'll handle everything for me?"

'I will,' he promised. Drawing his chair to the desk he worked a while with pencil and paper. 'That should do it,' he said, handing her the sheet covered with figures. She glanced at it and nodded.

'I won't bother to read it all. Whatever you say is all right with me.'

'Always?'

'Do you need to ask?'

SIXTEEN

Slade returned to the waterfront to supervise the activities there, but seven o'clock found him back in the Westport offices where he found Mack Russell staying late in case he might be needed. He sat down with Vera and awaited the arrival of the Grayson Line representative, who appeared shortly, an elderly man with a composed, authoritative manner. He shot Slade a keen glance, bowed to Vera.

'Miss Allen, I presume?' he said. 'Here is my card.'

Vera glanced at it and passed it to Slade. 'Sit down, Mr. Calvert,' she invited and gestured to her companion.

'Mr. Slade, my manager, will handle everything,' she added.

Calvert looked a little apprehensive as El Halcón's cold eyes met his; but Slade's smile quickly put him at his ease.

'I suppose we might as well get down to business, Mr. Slade,' he said. 'Now about the salvage settlement—'

'I don't think we will have any difficulty coming to terms, Mr. Calvert,' Slade interrupted. 'Here is what the Westport Company considers adequate compensation.'

The agent took the sheet on which Slade had worked earlier in the day, glanced at the sum in question, then stared, shifting his gaze to Slade. He hesitated, then, 'I must honestly say that under the laws of salvage, the courts would grant you much more,' he said.

'Perhaps,' Slade conceded. 'But there is something else to be considered—the law of decency. The Westport Company has no desire to profit unduly from your company's misfortune.'

The agent was not a man to waste words. 'Miss Allen, and Mr. Slade, in behalf of my company, I thank you,' he said. A smile brightened his rather somber countenance.

'And if you won't think I presume, I'd like to say that I personally thank you. It is refreshing to meet with people who still honor what some would call the old-fashioned virtues. And now if you will have the necessary papers drawn up, I will gladly sign them.'

Vera called to Russell in the outer office, whose typewriter at once began to click.

'And nothing has been heard of the captain and crew of the Albemarle?' Calvert asked.

'Nothing as yet,' Slade replied. The agent shook his head sadly.

'It is unexplainable, their abandoning the vessel that way,' he said. 'The captain was a trustworthy man, and so were his crew members. Something strange and, I greatly fear, terrible, must have happened.'

'Yes,' Slade agreed, with a grimness that was lost on the agent.

Soon everything was shipshape. Calvert shook hands with Slade, bowed to Vera.

'Miss Allen,' he said, 'I think I can safely assure you that my company will remember this act of generosity on your part, and that you will never have cause to regret it. Goodnight, it has been a great pleasure to know you both.' With a smile, and another bow, he took his departure.

'Yes,' Vera said to Slade, 'as usual, you were right.'

'Never kick a man when he's down,' the

Ranger replied. 'Help him to his feet and make a friend of him instead of an enemy. And you didn't do too bad.'

'I did darn well,' she declared. 'The Westport Company will be on easy street for a while.' She sprang to her feet.

'And now take me to dinner before I topple over. The Matagorda, of course. I want to thank the boys and assure them they'll get their share without delay.'

'Which will be good hearing for the waterfront saloons, and the waterfront girls,' Slade chuckled.

'Well, is there any better way to spend money than on a woman?' she retorted.

Slade chuckled again, and did not argue the point.

They found the Matagorda crowded, as usual. Shouts of greeting and a waving of hands heralded their entrance. Evidently the salvage of the Albemarle was still the chief topic of conversation. Bert, the owner, escorted them to the table he had reserved.

Glancing around, Slade saw that Captain Hawkins and most of the deckhands of the two Westport tugs were present. The Aransas men, so far as he could see, were conspicuous by their absence; apparently they had no stomach for the celebration.

After their dinner was finished, Slade rounded up the Westport hands and brought them to the table, where Vera thanked them for what they did and promised they'd receive their salvage money the next day. Pleasing information which was received with a bobbing of heads and grins of anticipation.

'Now they'll really let themselves go and all be busted by morning, knowing there is more on the way,' Slade said. 'Men have all the best of things,' Vera lamented. 'A girl can't let herself go that way, and get by with it.'

'Some do,' he returned. 'However, it's hardly what's expected from a respectable ship owner.'

Vera sniffed. 'Respectability has its drawbacks,' she declared. 'Sometimes I think I'd rather be a dance-floor girl. They don't have to bother too much about such things. And goodness knows they're popular enough.'

'Okay,' he replied. 'I'll speak to Bert and maybe he'll put you on.'

'I'm afraid you'd shock the poor dear into a stroke or something,' she giggled.

While Vera watched the dance-floor, Slade smoked, and reviewed the situation as it stood. With what he had accomplished as temporary manager of the Westport Company he was fairly well satisfied, as a Ranger he was not. True he had made some progress, but the main problem, that of bringing the band of sea-going outlaws to justice, still confronted him and seemingly defied solution. He hadn't a thing on anybody that would stand up in court.

Well, the old saying had it, 'Judge Colt holds court on the Rio Grande!' Perhaps a similar method might be applied with success in the Corpus Christi country.

Vera turned to face him. 'Let's dance,' she suggested. 'At least I can do that without creating a scandal.'

They had a couple of dances together and after the second Vera was a trifle breathless, for both numbers had been fast ones.

'Let's rest a while,' she said.

'Fine,' Slade agreed, 'I crave coffee.'

'Me, too,' she said. 'You don't drink much, do you, Walt?'

'Oh, I have a few snorts now and then, but coffee is my favorite tipple,' he replied.

'Mine, too,' she said. 'Seems we have something in common.'

'Is that all?' he asked, his eyes dancing. She smiled and dimpled.

'Well—no,' she admitted. Under the laughter in his eyes she blushed rosily.

The doors swung open and a group of cowhands filed in. *They* found places at the bar well within Slade's view. He at once recognized them for the Circle P bunch, Watson Payne's riders. Slade studied them as he sipped his coffee and gradually arrived at a conclusion.

They were a quite ordinary appearing bunch of rannies, nothing outstanding about any of them. Tobe Larsen, the range boss, who had the run-in with Del Gregory, showed indications of an irascible temper, but his countenance on a whole, Slade felt, was rather stupid. Capable of properly following a cow's tail, but that was about all. The same went for his companions.

No, Watson Payne's outlaw bunch was not made up of his cowhands, of that the Ranger now felt sure. Their operations bespoke daring, ruthlessness, intelligence. The group at the bar could, in his opinion, be salty enough did occasion warrant, doubtless did not lack courage, and were efficient in their own line of work. But when that was said, all was said.

Which gave the Ranger food for thought and caused him to arrive at a sudden decision.

Incidentally, there was no doubt but that the crews of the two Aransas tugs were of a much more formidable calibre and, Slade believed, were far from being typical deckhands. Very likely they were more than ordinarily capable at anything to which they might set their hands. And it was probable they had taken part in more than one type of activity. The hellion who drew the gun on him when he larruped the tug captain, Serge Bledsoe, knew how to handle an iron and it was instinctive for him to go for one in a moment of stress.

'Let's have one more before we go,' Vera suggested. So they danced another number, said goodbye to Bert and the others, and walked slowly uptown under the stars.

SEVENTEEN

The following morning, Slade did not approach the waterfront. Instead, he got the rig on Shadow and rode west. A mile or so from town he reined in and gazed back the way he had come until he was satisfied he was not leaving a trail. He could not be observed by anybody in the town. Then he turned from the trail and rode north by slightly west.

'Horse,' he said, 'I'm playing a hunch. Unless my memory plays me false, a few miles to the north is another trail, a very old trail that I imagine is hardly ever used anymore. Quite likely it was an Indian track in the beginning. It runs west, paralleling the bay shoreline. That's where we're headed for. Why?

'Because I'm pretty sure that Watson Payne has, in addition to his tugboat crews, six or seven riders, former cowhands. The robbery of The Western Express last month, and the Kingston stage the month before, was not committed by deckhands, that is sure for certain. Range riders on horseback perpetrated those outrages, and I'm ready to swear it was Payne's bunch.

166

'Well, if so, the hellions must have a hangout where they hole up between chores. They wouldn't live in town, for then their getting together would be noticed and occasion comment. When they want to visit Corpus Christi or Rockport, for instance, they'd slide in by ones or twos and attract no attention, sliding out the same way. I figure that their hangout should be up here somewhere in the brush and hill country, which provides plenty of cover. Not too far from town and the bay, and not too close. We're going to try and locate that hide-away. See?'

Shadow snorted noncommittally and wormed his way through the chaparral, avoiding thorns and obstructing branches with uncanny deftness.

El Halcón's aim was laudible, but putting it into effect was something else again. To try and locate an isolated hidden cabin or substitute shelter in this sea of towering brush that over-ran rises and hollows and deep dry washes was about like trying to root out a particular tick on a sheep's back. But Slade was optimistic nevertheless, for he had an ace in the hole.

As he anticipated, a few miles further on he came to the snake track that answered for a trail. The surface had been beaten hard by the tread of untold myriads of padding moccasins during the course of the years, until it absorbed little water. As a result, there was only a scattering of vegetation springing from the impervious crust.

Scanning the baked surface as he rode slowly, Slade shook his head from time to time at the negative results. After a while, he dismounted and crawled along the trail on hands and knees, his eyes close to the ground.

Shadow watched the proceeding with evident contempt. 'Delusions of grandeur!' his snort seemed to say. 'Thinks he's a horse!'

After perhaps a score of yards of painful progress, with Shadow pacing hesitantly behind, Slade turned and addressed him.

'Uh-huh, but for all your snorting and sneering, I found what I was looking for. Quite a few times, and recently, shod horses have passed this way, going and coming. Now what do you think of that?'

Shadow refused to comment; Slade mounted and rode on, slowly and watchfully, his eyes roving everywhere, his ears attuned to catch the slightest alien sound. There were places where he could not see a dozen yards ahead, and riders bulging around one of the brush-encroached bends would be on top of him before he sighted them.

Meanwhile he was counting heavily on his ace in the hole. His eyes constantly searched the sky for that indubitable evidence of human activity—smoke. Men have to eat, and they are not given to devouring raw food. Smoke rising against the sky signified that man was somewhere in the neighborhood, perhaps close at hand, perhaps miles away. But did the pale streamer continue long enough, it would guide the way and eventually bring him to the presence of its authors.

But the heavens remained serene. Occasional tufts of fleecy cloud drifted past in happy freedom. Once a lordly eagle breasted the upper winds, the sunlight glinting on his plumage, and once a flock of raucous crows winged north by east, cursing everything and everybody out of pure devilishness and causing Shadow to snort angrily.

Slade rode slowly but steadily, constantly scanning his surroundings, alert as he approached bends in the trail, of which there were many.

It was uneasy business. He was confident that the trail had been frequently used recently and there was no guarantee that somebody or somebodies might not be using it right now, which might well bode unpleasant consequences for himself.

The sun climbed the long slant of the eastern sky and when it crossed the zenith Slade knew that he was well past the reef from which Westport One hauled the stranded steamer. And still he had discovered no signs of human life, save the almost invisible hoof prints on the trail. And they could have been made by cowhands or others taking a short cut to some perfectly legitimate destination. He was beginning to wonder if his hunch was a straight one.

And when he was abruptly made to realize he was not alone in this apparently endless sea of brush, it was not through a tell-tale streamer of smoke, but by something much more alarming.

He had rounded the last of a series of bends when to his ears came a sound, a steady drumming that he instantly catalogued as the beat of fast hoofs, coming from behind. He whirled Shadow and sent him into the brush, heedless of thorns. He had barely rendered himself and the cayuse invisible from the trail to any but the most searching eyes when around the nearest bend careened four riders. As they swept past where Slade sat, scarcely daring to breathe, two cowhands appeared. Of the two riding in front, one was Serge Bledsoe, the Aransas tugboat skipper. The other, tall, erect, swaying gracefully to the movements of his mount, was Watson Payne. Without glancing back, they vanished around another bend a couple of hundred yards to the west.

*   *   *

Walt Slade found himself in a quandary as to his next move. To try to follow the unsavory quartette by sight or sound at the speed they

170

were going would be rank nonsense, and quite likely just a convenient way to commit suicide. Let them slow up after rounding one of the numerous bends and they would undoubtedly hear him coming and be all set to take care of him when he put in an appearance. And odds of four to one were a bit lopsided even for El Halcón. Payne and his followers were desperate men with no regard for the sanctity of human life.

So all he could do was drift along slowly with eyes and ears open and hope for an opportunity. Carefully he scanned the growth on either side as he rode, for it was logical to believe that his quarry would turn off somewhere.

But mile after mile the wall of growth continued unbroken. And eventually it *was* smoke that gave him the clue as to the whereabouts of the hangout, toward which the four riders were headed. Doubtless they had arrived there and were preparing a meal. He judged that the thin streamer of paler blue, rising against the sky, was perhaps two miles farther ahead. He slowed his pace and increased his vigilance.

When he caught the first pungent whiff of burning wood, he slowed Shadow to a crawl. A few hundred yards farther and there was a thinner patch of growth on the right. Into this he turned the cayuse and kept him going until, not far from the trail, he came to where the brush thinned still more and there was a scanty out-cropping of grass. He dismounted, tied the reins together and flipped out the bit. From his canteen he poured water into his cupped hands and gave the horse a drink.

'Okay, now you take it easy for a spell and keep quiet,' he told him. 'Can't risk your clumping any longer. Be seeing you.'

With which he wormed his way westward through the chaparral, in utter silence.

After a bit the growth began to thin again and Slade reduced his speed still more, until he was traveling about the rate of a rheumatic snail.

Stronger and stronger grew the smell of smoke. A dozen more crawling paces, and through a final fringe of chaparral, he sighted its source; a stick-and-mud chimney attached to a weatherbeaten but fight-looking cabin similar to many others encountered in the hill and brush country. Built by hunters, trappers, miners, or desert rats who craved solitude.

From where he peered out through the leafy screen he had a slantwise view of the shack, which was less than half a dozen yards distant, and sat in a small clearing. Over to one side was a leanto under which stood half a dozen horses, four of them still saddled and wearing nosebags. Evidently a couple more hellions had been awaiting the four he trailed. And to all apearances they did not intend to stay long.

The door of the cabin stood open, and from the interior came the rumble of voices and a clatter of dishes. Evidently a meal was in the course of preparation. A smell of frying meat and boiling coffee further attested to the fact.

Slade earnestly wished he could get a look into the cabin, but, conditions being what they were, this was impossible. He tried to peer through a window that faced toward him, but the panes were so streaked with dust that he could see nothing but moving shadows within. He waited, tense and expectant, for further developments.

Inside the cabin conversation languished to the near silence of hungry men eating. Knives and forks rattled. The wait grew tedious for the watcher in the brush.

Finally there was a scraping of pushed back chairs and the rumble of voices resumed. A few more minutes passed, then the tall figure of Watson Payne appeared in the doorway. Slade stiffened, utterly motionless, for it seemed to him that Payne's eyes were searching the growth where he stood. He realized a moment later, however, that the rancher's gaze was fixed on the brush farther to the west, beyond which was doubtless the trail.

For some moments Payne stood in the doorway, then abruptly he stepped out.

'Come on,' he called over his shoulder. 'We

can't wait any longer.' With long easy strides he headed for the leanto.

Five men filed out of the cabin, the last one banging the door shut. One was Bledsoe, two more Slade recognized as the riders who had accompanied Payne and the skipper. The other two were of the cowhand type with nothing outstanding about them, so far as the Ranger could see. All followed Payne to the leanto.

The nosebags were slipped off. Rigs were quickly cinched into place on the two unsaddled cayuses. All six men mounted and, Payne in the lead, rode across the clearing to strike the growth a bit to the right of where El Halcón stood motionless. The brush swallowed them. A moment later he heard the beat of hoofs on the hard surface of the trail, headed east at a fast pace.

Some hard thinking followed on the part of the Ranger. Reluctantly he discarded the notion of trying to follow Payne and his companions. By the time he got back to Shadow they would have a long head start, and he couldn't risk trying to draw near enough to keep them within sight or sound. Besides, he earnestly desired a look at the inside of the cabin. Perhaps it would reveal some clue as to their intentions or their former activities. He waited a little longer, then confident that they were not coming back for something they had forgotten, he left his place of concealment and approached the cabin.

He approached with caution, against the chance that another of the band, his horse grazing somewhere out of sight, might have been left behind, although he did not think that was the case.

Best not to take chances, however. Just outside the closed door he paused to listen.

No sound came from within, and the cabin had the 'feel' of an empty house. Standing well to one side, he reached out and pushed the door open. It swung back on creaking hinges. Slade shot a quick glance at the interior. There was nobody in sight.

Reassured, he stepped inside, surveying what met his eyes with interest, wrinkling his nose in distaste.

The cabin showed plenty of signs of continued tenancy. And more signs that the occupants were slovenly housekeepers. Tumbled blankets on bunks built against the walls looked filthy. A table was littered with dirty dishes. The floor was covered with cigarette butts, bacon rinds and egg shells. It was spotted and scummy with spilled grease.

In the big fireplace, a coffee pot steamed. Greasy skillets gave forth an odor of fried meat. The place boasted other odors, the least said about the better.

An open door led to a small and gloomier room that a brief inspection showed to have doubtless been used by the original builder as a storeroom, for it contained several rusty picks, a couple of shovels, also rusty, and four or five steel drills. The panes of its single window were so dirty that hardly any light filtered through.

There were plenty of staple provisions on shelves pegged to the walls, and tin cups and plates.

A scrap of paper propped against a half-filled coffee cup caught Slade's eye. On it was written in a very neat hand, doubtless Watson Payne's, the single word 'Ranchero.'

For several moments Slade stood turning the paper over and over in his fingers, racking his brain in search of what it might mean, for the name seemed to strike a familiar chord to his memory.

Abruptly he recalled why the name seemed familiar. Ranchero was the name of the steamer that plied from Corpus Christi to Brownsville and up the Rio Grande to Laredo. Now what the devil did *this* mean?

Suddenly he stiffened to an attitude of listening. Outside sounded a thudding of hoofs and a mutter of harsh voices. The hellions were coming back! He was trapped. His hands dropped to the butts of his guns and he shot a glance around the room. No chance to get out the window; the door was worse. There was but one thing to do, and a mighty unsatisfactory thing at that. He whirled and darted into the small and darker storeroom, drew both guns and waited.

EIGHTEEN

The outer door, which he had closed after entering, swung open. Crouched against the far wall of the little room, Slade saw two men enter. With a surge of relief he saw that they were not members of the party which rode away. Now he had it! The cryptic notation on the sheet of paper had been left as a message to these new arrivals. He remembered Payne calling to his companions that they couldn't wait any longer. Evidently he had been referring to the pair who had put in a belated appearance.

One of the men, both of whom were dressed as cowhands, picked up the paper from where Slade had dropped it on the table and peered at it.

'So that's it, eh?' he remarked to his companion. 'Looks like it's going to work out. We'll grab a bite to eat and then hightail. Payne'll be sore'n the devil if we're late. Liable to be sore anyhow, us not being here when he showed up. Blast it! a feller has a right to a drink now and then. Haul out some bacon and eggs—that'll be fast.' The pair got busy around the fireplace.

Meanwhile Slade was doing some hard and fast thinking. He could hardly remain where he was without being discovered. All that was needed was for one of the pair to glance through the door in his direction. Better to take the initiative; he could easily get the drop on them. Then he might be able to bluff them into doing a little talking to save their own unsavory hides. He really didn't have a thing on them—no law against holing up in an abandoned cabin that he'd ever heard of—but they didn't know it. Make them think that Payne and the others were already rounded up and had talked. A loco chance to take, all around, but better than gambling on the pair not sighting him. If they did, it would almost inevitably be a corpse and cartridge session. Right now the advantage would be with him. He glided to the door. His voice rang out, 'Reach! You're covered!'

The pair sprang erect as if prodded by hot irons, staring in stupefied amazement at the grim figure facing them. Their hands went up; there was nothing else they could do. They were fairly caught settin'!

Slade took a step forward, his lips opening to speak. His foot came down on one of the grease smears, he slipped, floundered off balance.

The pair took instant advantage of the mishap, their hands streaking to their holsters. The room rocked and quivered to the bellow of sixshooters.

A slug ripped Slade's sleeve, graining the flesh of his arm. Another sliced along his thigh, hurling him sideways with the shock. Ducking, weaving, he shot with both hands as fast as he could pull trigger. The smoke clouds rolled, the orange flashes darted back and forth.

Abruptly he realized there was nothing to shoot at. The two owlhoots lay sprawled on the floor, motionless. Slade lowered his guns and peered at them through the fog. Mechanically he ejected the spent shells from his Colts and replaced them with fresh cartridges. He cast another glance at the bodies. Well, he wouldn't get any information from *them*. At least not vocally; they'd tell no tales this side of Judgment Day.

Examination of his own hurts proved them to be trifling; a little antiseptic salve and they'd be okay. He was a bit shaken by the suddenness of it all and his mouth and throat were dry. So he rummaged a tin cup from one of the shelves, soused it in a bucket of water that stood nearby, and filled it with coffee from the still steaming pot. That helped, and a second drunk more slowly helped more. Rolling and lighting a cigarette, he leaned against the wall and decided on his next move.

First of all, the bodies must be gotten rid of, and all traces of his uninvited visit to the cabin removed. After which, the two horses must be taken care of. Then when the rest of the bunch returned, they would have no reason to suspect what happened and would doubtless assume that their missing companions had wandered off somewhere on some business of their own. They'd very likely be puzzled at their non-appearance but would hardly guess the truth.

Pinching out the butt and casting it among the numerous others that littered the floor, he examined the bodies. The faces, he thought, were vaguely familiar; he believed he had seen them somewhere in Corpus Christi, perhaps at the Matagorda. Didn't matter anyhow.

The pair's pockets revealed nothing of interest save a rather large sum of money, which he replaced. Sheriff Davis could take care of that when the proper time came.

One by one, he dragged the bodies from the cabin and into the denser growth, covering them with leaves and dead branches; they'd keep for a while, providing the coyotes didn't poison themselves by way of them. And he had a feeling that they wouldn't have to remain where they were for long. Yes, very likely the showdown wasn't far off.

Returning to the cabin, he made sure all was in order. There were blood stains on the floor, but they could hardly be noticed amid the grease spots and other litter. With a final glance around, he headed for the outside, pausing first to replace the scrap of paper against the coffee cup as it was when he discovered it. He left the cabin and closed the door.

Next in order were the horses. Those he would take with him and turn them loose not far from town, where they could reach grass and water and fend for themselves until somebody picked them up. There it wouldn't matter who sighted them; just so they were not found in the vicinity of the cabin.

First, however, he retrieved Shadow and rode him up the trail until he was opposite the cabin. Now that he knew what trail to look for, the turning-off point was plainly apparent. He carefully marked the location of the cabin and knew that with his plainsman's instinct for distance and direction he could find it again even on the darkest night.

With a glance at the sun, which was now close to the western horizon, he set out for Corpus Christi at a fast pace. He had little fear of meeting Payne and his bunch on the way, for he had an uneasy premonition that they were up to no good and were planning something that would keep them away from their hidden hangout for quite some time. He hoped he might be able to thwart whatever nefarious activity they had in mind, but was not optimistic. He urgently desired to consult with Sheriff Davis and Captain Si Hawkins at the earliest possible moment.

The led horses were good critters and,

unburdened, had no difficulty keeping up with Shadow who, although he was sifting sand, was not extending himself.

The sun sank behind the western hills, the dusk deepened, and the flaming scarlet and gold of the sunset sky faded to steel gray, to blue-black, silver studded with stars.

It was long past full dark when, a few miles west of Corpus Christi, he came upon a spot where the growth was thinner than average. Turning south, he threaded his way through it until he reached the main trail. There he removed the rigs from the led horses and tossed them into a thicket. Leaving the cayuses already grazing contentedly near the water's edge, he continued to town.

Arriving there, his first chore was to care for his horse. Then he hurried to the sheriff's office and had the good luck to find Davis in.

'Now what?' the old peace officer asked. 'You look like you've got something on your mind.'

'I have,' Slade replied. 'First off, what do you know about the steamer Ranchero?'

'Why, not too much,' Davis admitted. 'She makes the run from here to Laredo and back a couple of times a month.'

'What cargo does she usually carry?'

'Most anything,' the sheriff replied. 'I do happen to know that she sometimes brings a money shipment from Laredo to a Corpus Christi bank. That information ain't given out to the general public, though.'

'I see,' Slade observed dryly. He'd had some experience with the way 'secret' business of the sort was transacted. Not hard for an interested party with connections to learn the supposed secret. He was beginning to get the drift of things.

'And where is she now, have you any idea?' he asked. The sheriff shook his head.

'Might be anywhere between here and Laredo,' he replied.

Slade was silent a moment. Abruptly he rose to his feet. 'Come on,' he said, 'we're going down to the waterfront and see if we can learn anything from Si Hawkins; he usually knows what's going on and may be able to spot the Ranchero for us. I've a notion she's not far from Corpus Christi about now, somewhere out on the bay. I'll tell you everything a little later. We'll eat at the Matagorda. I haven't had anything but a cup of coffee since breakfast.

'Just a minute, though,' he added as they left the office. 'First we'll stop at the Westport offices and see if Vera may happen to be waiting for me there.'

Vera was, huddled in a chair. She sprang up with a glad cry when Slade entered.

'And I'm starving!' she wailed, after properly greeting him.

'We'll take care of that right away,' he promised. 'First, though, are the tugs in port?'

'I'm afraid not yet,' she replied. 'They headed for the east end of Mustang Island a while ago, where a ship is in some sort of trouble.'

Slade stifled an exasperated exclamation. His irritation was increased when they reached the waterfront and he saw that the space where the Aransas tugs were usually moored was also vacant.

'Let's eat,' he said, leading the way to the Matagorda. 'We'll try and get a table where we can talk.'

They were fortunate to find a table that was suitable. While awaiting their orders, Slade, speaking in a very low voice, acquainted his companions with the day's happenings. Vera gasped. The sheriff swore, under his breath. 'And you figure they might be aiming to try something against the Ranchero?' he asked.

'I don't know for sure, but I wouldn't be at all surprised,' Slade answered. 'Quite likely she'll be found "abandoned" tomorrow, with her crew missing. We'll do what we can to prevent it, but I'm afraid it won't be much. Now all we can do is wait for Hawkins to get in. He's the only one I'd trust with the chore I have in mind; if he can't pull it off, nobody can.

'I've a notion,' he continued, 'that Payne is getting a trifle jumpy. He may be planning to lie low for a while, or even pull out of the section, after one more good haul; the outlaw mind often works that way. The smarter specimens have an uncanny knack for sensing trouble and avoiding it. Take the Brocius gang over in Arizona, for example. They raised heck and shoved a chunk under a corner for quite a while, then disbanded and pulled out before anybody got sent to jail. Some went to Mexico, including Curly Bill himself, according to the story, and lived out prosperous and respectable lives.

'I've a notion, though,' he added grimly, 'that it is not going to be the case with *Señor* Payne and his hellions.'

Looking at his bleak face and icy eyes, Sheriff Davis was willing to agree.

*   *   *

It was nearing midnight when Slade recognized the deep-toned whistle of Westport One. He hurried out to see the Westport tugs steaming into port. He was up the gangplank and had contacted Captain Hawkins before it was fully in place. He drew the skipper aside.

'Si,' he said, 'have you any notion where the steamer Ranchero from Laredo should be about now?'

Hawkins considered a moment. 'Why, I'd say she's somewhere on the bay to the west of here,' he replied. 'That is if she kept to her schedule and course. Supposed to dock here tomorrow.'

Slade arrived at a quick decision.

'Si,' he said, 'have your boys grab something to eat and get ready to steam as soon as they can. Tell them that it will be double time for every hour they're out.'

Hawkins chuckled. 'For that sort of overtime the swabs will be ready to sail to China,' he declared. 'What's up?'

'As soon as you get them lined up, come to our table in the Matagorda and I'll let you know what I have in mind,' Slade answered. 'It's mighty important, and with luck you might be able to save some lives, although at the moment that is doubtful, I'll have to admit.'

'Be right with you,' Hawkins promised, and hurried off to give the orders to his men.

When Hawkins arrived at the table, Slade handed out the powders, terse and to the point.

'Try and locate the Ranchero. If she's steaming into port okay, fine! Just sort of convoy her in. Otherwise, keep looking till you find her, or what's left of her.'

Hawkins stared in astonishment. Slade told him everything, briefly.

As the skipper listened, his face flushed with anger, his eyes sparkled.

'The blasted pirates!' he growled. 'First thing, soon as I eat, I'm setting sail for my

186

room. I got a couple of good rifles there. I can shoot, and so can my mate.'

'Okay,' Slade agreed, 'but try not to get into trouble. If you sight the Aransas tugs, keep away from them; you'd be badly outnumbered. If you learn anything relative to the Ranchero, head back here as fast as you can and report to me. I'll be down here early this morning. Right now I'm going to try and knock off a few hours of shuteye. Davis, you'd better do the same; the devil only knows when we'll get a chance for some more.'

Hawkins fairly gulped down his meal. In short order, he and his deckhands trooped out and less than half an hour later, Westport One roared out of the harbor. Slade noted that the Aransas tugs had still not yet put in an appearance.

'Let's go,' he told Vera. 'See you later in the morning, Berne. Be all set to get a posse together pronto. Your three deputies and three or four more should be plenty.'

NINETEEN

It was well past noon when Westport One steamed into port. Captain Hawkins' face was grim when he reported to Slade.

'Yes, we found her,' he said. 'She's lying off Corpus Christi Pass, between Mustang and

Padre Islands. No crew aboard. Safe in captain's cabin had been blown open. Papers and other truck scattered about, nothing else. We put our House Flag on her and a man aboard. She ain't a derelict anymore, but our salvage.'

'Have Westport Three go put a line on her and bring her in,' Slade replied quietly. 'The sea is like glass and there's no wind; she should have no trouble handling her. You found just what I feared and expected. I hope to come even with those devils before so very many hours. You and your men grab off some sleep. And Si, I'm playing a hunch. Hire one of the off-duty fellows around here to keep the fire going and pressure up on Westport One.'

'You think—' Hawkins began.

'I'm not exactly thinking, just playing a hunch,' Slade interrupted. 'It could pay off. All set with everything? Okay, be seeing you, I hope.'

Hawkins saluted and hurried off to attend to his chores. Slade turned to the sheriff.

'Get your posse together,' he said. 'We're riding.'

'To that shack in the brush you told me about?' Davis asked as they headed uptown.

'That's right,' Slade answered. 'I feel fairly confident they'll be there for a while.'

'What became of the Aransas tugs, I wonder,' remarked the sheriff. 'Hawkins didn't see anything of them.'

'They'll be making port before long and, of course, knowing nothing.'

'Think they might try to salvage the Ranchero?'

Slade shook his head. 'They got all they wanted from the Ranchero, the chances are,' he said. 'As you told me last night, sometimes she packed as much as fifty thousand dollars in a bank shipment. Chances this trip was one of her big ones. No, they wouldn't make a try for the salvage, in my opinion, even if we didn't have our House Flag and a man aboard, which precludes any chance of another outfit horning in. To do so they'd have to do away with our representative on the Ranchero, and that would be just a mite obvious. So we'll get all set and amble west. No hurry. We've either got plenty of time or none at all, and I'd prefer to reach the cabin after dark; that should give us the advantage of surprise, and we'll need all the breaks we can get; it's a desperate outfit. I'm going to stop and see Vera for a few minutes, then we'll grab off a bite to eat and ride.'

TWENTY

An hour later the posse, eight strong, headed west, Slade setting the pace. After a while he turned north through the growth, and they reached the old trail without mishap. Again they rode steadily west.

Already the sun was low in the western sky, and before long it had dipped below the horizon. The posse continued through the deepening gloom. Slade studied the brush on either side, estimated distances. Now he rode very much alert, for there was a chance that the quarry might double back.

But the winding trail stretched on and on, silent and deserted. After a bit Slade slowed the pace. And now he was using his nose as well as his eyes and ears. Overhead the stars glimmered, with occasional driftings of fleecy clouds. And still only the call of a night bird broke the silence, against which the drumming of the horses' irons beat back as from an invisible wall.

And it was his nose that ultimately told him they were nearing their goal. To his sensitive nostrils came the unmistakeable pungent whiff of burning wood. The wind blew very gently from the west and he knew that the source of the smell could not be far ahead. He slowed the pace still more and finally called a halt.

'I think we're pretty close,' he told his companions, his voice little above a whisper. 'Here we'll shove the horses into the brush and leave them. I'm fairly sure that a short distance from the trail is a cleared space with grass. They won't stray.'

He was correct in his estimate. Less than fifty yards of slow and hard going and they did reach a spot where the chaparral was but scattered patches with grass growing between. Here he dismounted, motioning the others to do likewise.

'From here on we travel by shank's mare,' he whispered. 'Take it slow and easy and for Pete's sake don't make a noise. If they catch on, we'll get a reception we won't like. Less than a hundred yards to go. Come on.'

With El Halcón leading and moving with the silence of a drifting shadow, the posse stole forward on the heels of their leader, emulating him as best they could, carefully moving branches aside, planting their feet cautiously so as to break no dry and fallen twigs, to kick no stone.

'I think we can make it to the door without being spotted,' Slade breathed. 'From the smell, I judge they've been preparing a meal and with good luck we may catch them at the table. Right through the door after me, and if they don't give up—and very likely they won't—shoot fast and shoot straight. You do the talking, Berne; you're sheriff of the county.'

Another score of yards and he abruptly halted. Directly beyond a final fringe of leaves was the cabin, light glowing murkily through its dirty windows. Slade waited until the others were abreast of him. Then he crossed the open space with quick, light steps, the posse crowding behind. Coming opposite the closed door he turned, raced ahead and hit the door with his shoulder. It banged open and he was in the room, the posse surging after him.

Seated at the table were six men, knives and forks in their hands. One was Serge Bledsoe. Another was Watson Payne. They stared open mouthed at the unexpected intruders. Sheriff Davis' voice blared at them, 'Elevate! In the name of the law!'

For an instant it seemed the outlaws would surrender without a shot fired. Then Watson Payne acted with bewildering speed. Over went the table, the dishes flying in every direction. Payne's right hand shot forward, his double barreled derringer spatting against his palm. Before he could pull trigger, Slade drew and shot. The derringer spun through the air. Payne gave a howl of anger. From behind the overturned table gushed orange flashes. Through the tumult of dodging figures and swirling smoke, Slade saw Payne dash for the small, inner room. He strove to get past the

utter confusion boiling in front of him, but
before he could make it, there was a terrific
crackling of breaking glass and splintering
wood work. Payne had gone through the
window. And for the moment El Halcón had
his hands too full to attempt pursuit.

The outlaws, some partially sheltered by
the overturned table, fought like cornered
rats. But taken off balance, bewildered by the
suddenness of the onslaught, they never had a
chance. In a moment, three were stretched
motionless on the floor. The remaining two,
one of them Bledsoe, had their hands in the
air and were howling for mercy.

'Hold it!' Slade shouted. 'We want that pair
alive. Is anybody badly hurt?'

Three members of the posse had suffered
bullet wounds, none of them serious. Slade
decided they could take care of each other's
injuries.

'Tie them up,' he ordered, gestering to the
surrendered outlaws. Two possemen hurried
forward and did so.

Sheriff Davis was cursing like a madman.
'But the big he-wolf of the pack got away!' he
raved. 'Payne ain't here.'

'Yes, he got away,' Slade replied. 'Went
through the window of that other room. I
heard his horse's irons hit the trail. Doesn't
matter; I'm pretty sure I know where he's
heading for, and we'll be right on his tail. You
come along with Berne and me, Ray, and you,

Cooney. That'll be enough. The rest of you bring the prisoners to town and lock them up. I've a notion you'll find most of the money taken from the Ranchero around here somewhere. Perhaps you can *persuade* the prisoners to tell you where it is.'

'You're darned right we can!' growled one of the possemen, who was nursing a bullet gashed cheek and appeared in anything but a good temper. He glared at Bledsoe, who cringed away from his baleful stare.

'Come on, boys,' Slade told Davis and the other two, 'we're heading for Corpus Christi as fast we can get there. Be seeing the rest of you.'

He led the way to where the horses waited. Ten minutes later they were racing east along the trail.

'I'm playing a hunch,' he told his companions. 'A hunch that Payne will grab one of the tugs, load both crews on it, and take off for Mexico. There they would find sanctuary without any trouble. That's why I ordered Captain Hawkins to have steam up on Westport One and be all set to go. If things work out right, they won't have much of a start on us, and if we manage to keep them in sight I think Westport One can make better speed than either of their tubs. Anyhow, that's the way we'll play the hand.'

'And I got a notion ours is full of trumps,' said Davis. 'You sure figured it smart; I'd have never thought of it.'

'Just logical deduction,' Slade replied smilingly.

'Uh-huh, El Halcón deduction,' Davis chuckled.

As they sped along the winding track, Slade estimated the distance they covered. Abruptly he said, 'I think we're just about opposite that burned-over stretch of chaparral to the south. We'll turn off here and make for the lower trail. The going will be easier there and we'll have a better chance to cut Payne's lead.'

They turned their horses south, shoving them through the thorny growth. Slade's guess proved to be a straight one. Less than a mile of going and the horses' irons were kicking up puffs of ash, and all about were scorched trunks with leafless branches with the twigs burned away. Here they made much better speed and shortly reached the lower trail.

After allowing the horses a few minutes for a breather, Slade increased the pace. Soon the lights of Corpus Christi twinkled in the distance.

'Straight for the waterfront,' he directed. 'I've a notion we are going to get there in time.'

A few minutes later they were clattering through the almost deserted streets. As the horses' irons thudded on the floor boards of the wharf, opposite the Matagorda, Slade uttered an exclamation.

'There she goes!' he said.

In the distance, her funnel belching sparks and reddish smoke, a single tug was booming toward the pass between the two islands. A glance showed Slade that the other Aransas tug was lying at the wharf, looking lonely and deserted.

'Both crews aboard that one and headed for Mexico,' he added, gesturing toward the departing tug.

Even as they dismounted, Westport One's blower cut loose with a roar. 'Hawkins has steam up and is rarin' to go,' Slade chuckled.

Attracted by the tumult, men were streaming from the Matagorda across the way. Slade recognized Bert's mustache.

'Come here, Bert!' he called. The owner lumbered across to him.

'Take care of the horses, will you, Bert?' he requested. 'I'll do it,' Bert promised. 'Good huntin'!'

Up the gangplank, which was rising under their feet, hurried the posse. Hawkins met them on the deck. 'All set,' he said. 'After them? right!'

Slade took the wheel. He was confident his eyes could keep the fleeing tug in sight. He spun the spokes, circled Westport One from the pier, rang for full speed ahead. The exhaust bellowed, the propellor thrashed the water to foam, and away she went in the wake of the Aransas tug. The race was on!

'We'll catch her before she makes Mexico,' he confidently told the others who were grouped beside him. 'I'm sure we can make the better speed.'

'You're darn right we can!' Hawkins growled.

'We'll be outnumbered when the showdown comes, but I've a notion we'll be able to sort of even the odds in a hurry,' Slade added.

'I've got a rifle, and so has Paddy,' Hawkins put in. 'And we ain't no snides when it comes to shooting.'

'Six good shots should make it,' Slade predicted cheerfully. 'Say! that old tub is making speed, all right, but we're gaining a little all the time.'

In surprisingly short order they were through the pass and on the open sea. Slade could still see the dark smudge that was the Aransas tug, her phosphorescent wake and an occasional spark from her stack.

After a bit, however, he peered forward with narrowed eyes. 'She's pulling away from us,' he announced. 'I've a notion she has her safety valve tied down.' He glanced at Hawkins.

'Think *we* can risk it?' he asked.

'We got a brand-new boiler and I figure it'll take it,' the skipper replied cheerfully. 'If it don't, well—'

He hurried to the engine room. Soon he

was back.

'Tied down tight,' he announced. 'The boys there are singing,

> "High flying Skua Gulls!
> And Davy Jones' locker O" '

Slade chuckled; under the circumstances, the chantey was quite apt.

Now Westport One was quivering from stem to stern. Her stack was thundering, her plates creaking. Slade knew the pressure gauge was far above safety. They were taking a chance, even with a new boiler. But with grim satisfaction he saw that the distance between the two straining vessels was lessening.

'We're doing it,' he told his companions. 'In less than an hour, I'd say, we'll lay her aboard.'

'The sooner the better,' growled Sheriff Davis. 'I'm itchin' to line sights with those murdering devils. The Ranchero must have carried a crew of nine or ten.'

Half an hour passed, and the Aransas tug looked larger and larger. But now from the over-pressured boiler came an eerie whine that slowly shrilled, the plaint of tortured metal. Captain Hawkins made no sign. Neither did Slade. He estimated the distance. Already within long rifle range.

He was right. A moment later something

sang overhead. A second slug thudded against the hull plates. A third knocked splinters from the rail. The deckhands and the posse sought splinters beneath the bulwarks, but Slade stood erect, deftly spinning the spokes of the wheel, heedless of the death spitting at him from the darkness ahead, and roaring at him from the straining boiler. If the darned thing would just stay together a little longer they would come to grips with the outlaws.

'Anyhow, the flashes provide good steering way,' he remarked to grim old Captain Hawkins, who stood stolidly beside him.

'Helps some,' agreed the skipper. 'We'd oughta be able to do a mite of answering before long.'

'Yes—' Slade began. The words were wiped from his lips. Ahead the sea was lighted by a blinding glare followed by a thundering roar as the Aransas tug blew up with a tremendous explosion. Hawkins was knocked to the deck by the concussion. Slade reeled, steadied himself. In the blaze of light he saw timbers and huge chunks of steel and what looked to be the bodies of men flying through the air. Madly he spun the spokes to circle the tug away from the wreckage strewn in the water ahead.

'Ease her!' he shouted to Hawkins, who had scrambled to his feet. 'Ease her before we go to join those hellions, whereever they've gone.'

Hawkins raced to the engine room. A few moments later the safety valve rose to a screeching howl.

'What happened?' Sheriff Davis yelled above the tumult.

'Her boiler busted!' Hawkins bellowed back.

Slade was still circling the tug. He dared not approach too near the vicinity of the stricken vessel in the black dark that had swooped down.

Not that there was much use to approach; it was highly unlikely that any of the tug's occupants had survived the explosion. He glanced eastward. There was a rosy glow near the horizon.

'Be getting light enough to see in ten minutes or so,' he said.

The glow in the east brightened. The stars dwindled to needle points of steel, pricking through the robe of Night, and vanished. A pale radiance stole across the surface to the sea. Where the Aransas tug had been was only tossing water. Death strode across the waves and the rising mists, Slade thought, might well be the souls He had garnered.

With a last glance around, he spun the wheel, turned the tug's bow north by east and motioned to the helmsman to take over. Suddenly he was very, very tired.

'Cook's got coffee hot in the galley,' Hawkins said to him. 'I've a notion a cup will do you good.' Slade gratefully accepted the invitation.

After drinking the coffee, he rolled a cigarette and relaxed as he smoked, feeling a bit better. El Halcón was used to death, but not in such wholesale fashion and in such frightful shape.

'Well, anyhow it saved the county burying expense,' Davis remarked with grisly humor as he set down his empty cup. 'And sorta evens the score for the Ranchero and the Albemarle and others. The Good Lord don't need much to work with when He figures it's time to rid the earth of some varmints—just a little water vapor.'

Slade went on deck. The brilliant sunshine and the sparkling blue water helped. He breathed deeply of the pure air. Anyhow, the chore he had been sent to do was completed. Which also helped. Soon he was his normal cheerful self.

As the tug danced along, he pondered the vagaries of the outlaw mind, which always seemed to defeat its own ends. Had Watson Payne stuck to his illegitimate salvage operations he might well have gotten by indefinitely, for the scheme was almost foolproof. But the temptation of a big and quick haul was too much for him and had been his undoing.

The robbery and murder of Malcolm Henderson, the Westport purchasing agent, was another example of the callous greed that is the mainspring, and the weakness, of the criminal nature. Providing as it did the first real lead, which the Ranger followed slowly and tediously to a successful consummation.

When they arrived at Corpus Christi they found the other deputy awaiting them in the sheriff's office.

'Bledsoe talked,' he announced. 'Told us everything. Yes, they did for the Ranchero and the Albemarle and those other two ships supposed to be abandoned. They got plenty from the Ranchero, better'n forty thousand dollars. We found most of it in the cabin. Reckon Payne took the rest of it to Hades with him.

'Seems Payne was brought up as a rancher, over around the Sabine River country, but went to sea. Had a small smuggling ship working the coastwise trade and did mighty well with it. Hit on the wrecking and salvage notion and figured it would pay better than smuggling; reckon it did. Those hellions who worked the tugs were part of his smuggling ship's crew. The others were side-winders who handled the land end of his smuggling business. Oh, yes, some of the boys rode over to root out those two carcasses you hid in the brush, Mr. Slade. Guess they'll hold an inquest on all five tomorrow. If there's anything else you want to know about, reckon you'd better talk to Bledsoe.'

'I think we've heard enough for the time being,' Slade said. 'See you later, Berne; I'm going to look up Vera and give her the lowdown on what happened.'

'And just as you figured,' the deputy added as Slade turned to go, 'the Circle P cowhands weren't mixed up in the crooked business—didn't know a thing about it going on.'

Slade nodded. 'That, of course, was Payne's reason for using the old miner's cabin as a hangout for his bunch. Soon as I stumbled onto that I was sure his range riders were innocent.'

'And the same goes for the crews of his two steamers, according to Bledsoe,' the deputy concluded. ' 'Pears he kept them in strictly up-and-up coastwise trade.'

Slade nodded again. 'Guess it'll be up to the county authorities to try and untangle his affairs and decide what is to be done with his assets,' he observed to Sheriff Davis. 'Might be a good notion to turn the ranch over to the Circle P cowhands and the ships to the crews. Chances are, though, there'll be a lot of litigation before the business is straightened out. Be seeing you.'

Three days later Shadow, saddled and bridled, stood in front of the little house on Gavilan Street. Vera Allen walked slowly down the path with Slade.

'Yes, I'll have to be getting back to the post

and report to Captain Jim, and see what next he's got lined up for me,' he said. 'But we won't make it goodbye. Just *Hasta Luego.*'

'*Hasta Luego,*' she repeated. 'Till we meet again!'